THE
ROMA'S
LIES

THE ROMA'S LIES

SHAE COON

4 Horsemen
Publications, Inc.

4 Horsemen
Publications, Inc.

4 Horsemen Publications, Inc.
1497 Main St. Suite 169
Dunedin, FL 34698
4horsemenpublications.com
info@4horsemenpublications.com

Cover and Typesetting by 4 Horsemen Publications, Inc.
Edited by Tilda M. Cooke

Library of Congress Control Number: 2023936439

Paperback ISBN-13: 978-1-64450-977-7
Audiobook ISBN-13: 978-1-64450-980-7
Ebook ISBN-13: 978-1-64450-979-1

DISCLAIMER

This book is for mature readers only,
18+. It includes rough sexual scenes,
intense and humiliating punishments,
violence, criminal elements, and men-
tions of trafficking. Reader discretion
is advised.

TABLE OF CONTENTS

 The Roma's Lies

1

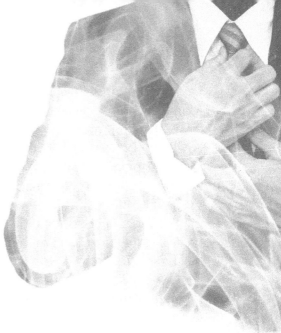

2007
The Home of Idris Calvano in Rome, Italy
Camil Radu

"How am I supposed to know? This machine has two dozen buttons on it." I gesture at the state-of-the-art washing machine.

"Then you should have asked, you stupid girl."

"I am not stupid!" I growl and fist my hands at my side.

"You should thank the Virgin Mary for being blessed with beauty because you do not have the brains. Not that you will need them when you're pawned off to some low-level member of the *famiglia*." She's speaking more to herself than me. Still, I hear her, and it riles my temper.

"At least I qualify to be in the *famiglia*," I smart off, then cringe when the haughty comment echoes back.

I am not that person—a selfish, entitled little princess. Mama and Papa are probably rolling in their graves at my bratty comment.

"Don't be so sure, girl. *Signore* Calvano may have different plans for you." Her words cause dread to pool in the pit of my stomach.

"What is that supposed to mean?"

"Nothing." The bitter old hag shrugs, and I know there's something that I'm missing—something Lolita has heard firsthand or through one of the other servants she has under her thumb and bullies into spying for her. "I would just watch that temper of yours. Even if *Signore* allows you to marry one of the men in the *famiglia*, sooner rather than later, that temper of yours will get you silenced ... permanently." She smiles deviously, exposing her nicotine-stained teeth.

I go to speak when his angry voice echoes down the hall to where we stand bickering. "Camil! Where the fuck is that skinny, little——"

"I'm in here, Don Calvano," I announce, and Idris turns the corner just in time for Lolita to shove the laundry basket full of his clothes into my arms.

"What the fuck did you do?" he shouts when he sees that his once-white undershirts are now a colorful array of blues and pinks—thanks to me.

"She took it upon herself to——"

"I wasn't speaking to you," he sneers in disgust at Lolita, and she bows her head in subservience.

Why does she get so hot and bothered by this asshole? If he ordered her to her knees and demanded she bark like a dog, she would.

SMACK!

2

I cry out and tumble over the small folding table when Idris backhands me. My cheek is on fire, but it's the large insignia ring on his pinky finger that has me seeing stars. I've never been hit before. Emil, Boian, and I used to rough-play when we were kids, but they never laid a hand on me in violence. Even my parents, who had every right to administer corporal punishment, never gave me more than a warning glare or the occasional grounding. So, to be the recipient of Idris's violent reaction has me stunned into silence.

He adjusts the cuffs of his shirt. "You will pay for every shirt you ruined. How many were there, Lita?" he addresses her where she stands, unperturbed by what she just witnessed.

"Six, *Signore.*"

Fucking snitch.

"Six shirts at two-hundred euros a piece..." He trails off, waiting for me to answer, but my lip is bleeding and swelling with every thump of my pulse.

When I don't answer, he dives his hand into my hair and yanks me to my feet. "Cat got your tongue, little Cami?" he taunts with the nickname my father used for me when he was alive, and tears sting my eyes at the reminder that I am all alone in this world. My parents are dead, and Emil and Boian left to serve in the Italian forces––left me.

Idris's fist tightens in my hair as he drags me through the palatial mansion, out the front door, and onto the gravel driveway where a dozen of his men stand, legs shoulder width apart, backs ramrod straight with hands behind them. As we approach, I can see Dante, my only protector in this place, lying on his back on the ground, groaning as he holds an arm that hangs from his shoulder in an unnatural position.

I'm tossed to the ground, my knees screaming in pain when the small gravel digs into my skin. "Say your goodbyes to this *traditore* (traitor) before I put a bullet in his head." I slowly lift myself and wobble on my feet when my head swims.

"Wha... What did he do?" I ask through the tears stuck in my throat. The tears that I refuse to shed in front of this *bastardo*.

"I said say your goodbyes, not question me."

I look back at the man who has become my guardian angel. "He's going to sell——"

BANG!

The muzzle of the gun in Idris's hand is still smoking when he turns his soulless eyes to me. "I gave you a chance to say goodbye." He points to Dante's corpse. "Let that be a lesson to you, girl. Anyone who goes against a Calvano will be met with brutal punishment and a bullet in their skull. Now, help my men clean up this mess." He holsters his weapon and leaves us to dispose of Dante's lifeless body.

Two soldiers lift Dante from the pool of blood seeping into the gravel. One catches my gaze. "Get to work, girl. Do a good job, and maybe I'll reward you after everyone goes to bed," he says lecherously and licks his cracked lips, not bothering to hide the way his beady eyes crawl over my underdeveloped fifteen-year-old body.

"Shut the fuck up and move, Nico. This bastard is heavy," the soldier, whose name I don't remember, grouses, but when they start moving again, he gives me an indiscernible nod.

A water hose is set beside my feet, and water comes gushing out, soaking the last pair of shoes I own that aren't worn through with holes. I stand there motionless, watching them carry Dante toward the outbuilding they use to liquefy the bodies.

When all three men disappear behind the heavy steel door of the building and I still haven't moved, someone pushes my shoulder from behind, and I turn to see Lolita smiling down at me with a look of victory painting her craggy face.

"You heard, *Signore:* clean up this mess." She jerks her chin up in superiority.

I pick up the hose, spray the gravel, and watch Dante's blood turn crimson to muted red. It takes me the rest of the afternoon and into the evening to rid the gravel driveway of blood.

The entire time, I don't shed a tear.

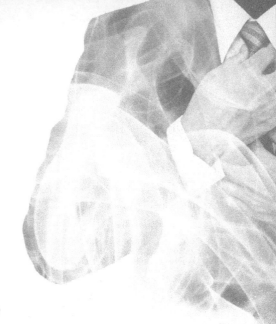

2

2012
Sinaloa, Mexico
Boian Greco

"What the fuck is taking so long, Sergeant Greco?" the captain bitches for the hundredth time over my comms, his Texas accent thick––though easier to understand after being under his command for nearly five years.

"I'm double checking the house," I answer with an indignant growl as I scan the Sinaloa compound with my heat vision binoculars. They've been glitching for the last twenty minutes, the heat signatures going in and out. What does the man want? I'm not about to blow the shit out of a compound that houses enslaved women and children without being absolutely sure they're all out safely.

"For fuck's sake. I swear to Christ—I'll require balls the size of melons in the next batch. Or maybe I should just keep to American products."

I roll my eyes. The "batch" he's referring to are lethal mercenaries who aren't afraid to get their hands dirty for the greater good—skilled killers, brutal, and unremorseful.

Mercenaries like me.

Emiliano and I enlisted into the Italian military forces straight out of high school. While Emil was content with staying with the ISAF, patrolling, peace-keeping, and so on, I craved something on the darker side. The kind of missions you were lucky to come back from alive––a source of contention between me and a silver-eyed siren back home in Rome.

Camilla Radu is Emil's and my childhood friend–– though she isn't a child anymore. She often wrote to Emil and me and would enclose a photo of her-self on her birthday each year. I watched her grow from the skinny, awkward thirteen-year-old girl I left behind to the eighteen-year-old woman with mouth-watering curves and the classic Italian beauty she was now. And fuck if I didn't have to talk my dick down at seeing her photo.

"Just blow the damn thing, so we can get out of this shit stain of a city," the captain grumbles.

"We're sure that the women and children are out?" I flip the switch to ready the charge.

"I told you the count three times, Greco. Now. Blow. It," he orders. With a heavy sigh, I press the button. Half a second later, the sky lights up like New Year's Eve in Italy. The ground rumbles below me where I lay hidden in the sparse foliage, far away enough not to be hit by debris but close enough to feel the heat of the blast. The sound of destruction

7

soothes the beast inside, and the demons are imprisoned in the cell of my past once again.

"Mission accomplished. I'm heading back." I gather my gear and tools to head back to HQ.

Three flesh traders down, thousands more to go.

The photo hovers above my face while I attempt to decompress. Tracing her eyes, smile, and curves with my eyes have my nerves firing on all cylinders and my dick begging for attention. I'm a sick bastard for my tawdry thoughts over a barely legal Camil, but I'll be damned if I can stop myself.

"Greco," one of the guys on my team yells from the open flap of my Temper tent. "Captain wants to see you."

"Now?"

"Now."

"Fucking hell." I pull myself up with a grunt and tuck Camil's photo into the *Spanish for Dummies* book she sent me last year. I throw on a shirt as I walk out into the hot evening air and head to the control tent, where the "boss" calls me after every mission.

Captain Phips's voice can be heard before I get two yards from my tent. "I understand what you're saying, sir, but——"

"But nothing, Phips!" the boss bellows through the phone speaker. "This was supposed to be quick and clean. You got the quick part, but you royally fucked up the clean part. What part of no women and children did you not understand?"

I freeze in place right outside the control tent door. Women and children? Fuck. Please don't tell me...

"Sir, I wasn't the one on scouting duty, but I assure you the man that was will be disciplined for his fuck up."

The man on scouting duty——meaning me.

I charge into the tent, and the look of fear on the captain's face tells me that he knows I heard him throw me under the bus. "Sir, this is Sergeant Boian Greco. I was——"

"Sir, I have to let you go. I'll call you when it's done." The captain disconnects the call and watches me hesitantly where I stand fuming.

"When what's done, Captain? When you're done torturing me for a fuck up you were instrumental in?"

"The numbers came straight from your scouting logs, Sergeant."

"And you assured me that all twenty of them got out before I blew the fucking place to hell!" I roar. "How many? How many did I kill?" I ask with deadly calmness.

The captain runs a trembling hand over his salt and pepper scruff and moves behind the desk to use it as a barrier. "Three," he answers, and like a lion let loose from its cage, I pounce. The metal table goes flying, and I have the captain by the throat and his feet dangling in mid-air as I lift him by his throat.

"Three? Can you not fucking count? You knew there were still victims in there, and you *still* ordered me to blow it?" I squeeze his throat tighter, and he

9

grapples at my hand, but I have at least four inches and thirty pounds of muscle on him.

"They ... weren't ... victims," he chokes under my hold.

I drop him back on his feet and fist his collar. "What do you mean? I heard the boss with my own ears. Women and children. Explain."

"All the women and children we went to rescue got out, but the fucker had his wife and kids at the compound. I couldn't risk not getting the victims out to grab his piece of filth family."

He might as well have hit me with a sledgehammer. I stumble back, eyes wide, heart thundering in my chest. Bile rises to my throat, and tears prick the back of my eyes. "You knew a woman and her children were in that compound and took it upon yourself to be their judge, jury, and executioner?"

"I did what needed to be done, Greco. If we went back into that compound for *some la concha de tu madre's*, motherfucker's family. It would have cost us the mission, and there would be a shit ton of pissed-off mercenaries banging down my fucking door demanding their payday that wouldn't have come!" he finishes with a huff of annoyance.

I take a threatening step forward, and he trips over his feet and stumbles into the filing cabinet to escape me. "Fuck the money! You're not God. You don't get to decide who lives and dies."

"What the hell do you think we've been doing, Greco?" The bastard has the balls to laugh. "With each mission, we do exactly that, and last I checked, you receive a paycheck just like the rest of us," he sneers.

"I don't give two shits about the money, and I don't kill innocent—"

"Of course, you don't care about the money. You've got your mafia buddy Calvano to line your pockets. Well, we ain't all so lucky, asshole. Now the question is are you gonna keep bitching like a little girl, or will you nut up and help us take these bastards down?" The edge of his lip tips up knowingly. He thinks he has me because he knows why I joined this particular team. They were known to go into the roughest areas and battle some of the most dangerous men in the world. It was like the purest heroin to an addict. But unlike an addict, I'm not willing to sacrifice innocence for my fix.

I unbuckle my gun holster and lay it on the filing cabinet by his head. "I'm out," I say, then walk out of the command tent.

I enter my tent, bumping shoulders with David, our sniper from Texas. "Whoa, Gecko, you nearly dislocated my shoulder," he jokes and rotates his shoulder.

"Stop fucking calling me that," I grumble, grabbing my rucksack, and start shoving the few clothes I have into the camo canvas bag.

"What? It's your call sign. I kind of gotta use it sometime. What the hell's going on? You being shipped off to another team? Cause if so, I'll go tear the captain a new—"

"I'm quitting," I say and grab the box of letters from Camil and her photo, gently placing them in the hidden pocket in my ruck I'd sewed in myself.

"The fuck you just say? You're quitting? Wow, I never thought I'd see the day the great Boian fucking Greco turn quitter." David shakes his head in disgust, and I'm on him before he can wipe the look of judgment from his face.

I fist his army Tee and bring him nose-to-nose with me. "You don't know shit, Winters. I have enough blood on my hands without getting paid to bathe in it. Now get the fuck out, and don't come back until I'm gone." I toss him aside and pick up my ruck.

"Fucking gladly," he mumbles before stomping out of my tent.

I scan my area to ensure I have everything, then walk out with the intention of never looking back.

But what's the old saying? Never say never...

3

Undisclosed location in the Swiss mountains
Present day
Camil

S witzerland is beautiful. It looks like a scene straight out of a Disney movie with its towering snowcapped mountains, fresh streams with glistening icicles that cling to the water's edge, and the small, pitched roof cabins dotting the snowy hillside where Boian's Swiss home stands sentry over the surrounding houses—a king among men.

Yes, it is a beautiful place—a dream for any woman to visit. And that's the crux of it. I'm not here visiting, and I don't get to go into town to explore the little shops or get to know the townspeople. In fact, I'm not allowed off the property because I'm a prisoner of Boian's making, one that he justifies under the guise of protecting me. It's all bullshit. I'm a nobody in the Calvano household. Yes, Emil and I are like brother and sister, and neither of us would hesitate to slits anyone's throat who tries to hurt the other, but no one outside the household knows that. Even the extended members of the *famiglia* didn't see me as more than just the help, so there is no point in hiding me away. Boian just wants me out of the way.

The capsule filled with the powerful sleep agent slides apart easily. I tip the contents into Dom's orange juice and watch the acidic fruit juice quickly dissolve the powder. It's the third one, and I can only pray he doesn't taste the bitter medicine.

Dom's been my bodyguard, aka babysitter, for weeks, but we've known each other since we were kids. As one of Emiliano Calvano's most trusted soldiers, he was assigned to watch over me after Greta ran away and was ultimately kidnapped. I didn't mind so much, really.

What I do mind, however, is being sent away by the man I grew up with, shared my deepest fears with, and love down to my bones, but that doesn't love me––so he says. Literally. The one time Emil asked Boian if he was in love with me, Boian didn't hesitate to deny having any feelings for me other than what a brother would have for a little sister.

Lies.

You don't look at a sister the way Boian looks at me. You don't *touch* the way he touches me in the rare moments he allows himself to. And you certainly don't kiss the way he kissed me at his welcome home party. It was years ago, but I can still feel the tingle in my lips, the bruising grip of his hands on my thighs as he lifted me against the unforgiving surface of one of the boulders along Emil's Olbia home. The way his cock pulsed behind the denim of his pants and the sound of my heartbeat thump, thump, thumping in my ears as he ravished me––only to shatter when he pulled away, dropped my legs to the floor, and walked away, never to acknowledge our moment again.

"Good morning," Dom greets me, and I return it by offering him the tainted orange juice with a smile. I should feel bad—and I do to a certain degree—but there's no other way he's letting me out of this house without him. "Thanks." He takes the offered glass and gulps it down in seconds.

"You're welcome. Do you want anything to eat? I can cook something up, or we can get something from the bakery up the road."

"Cabin fever?" Dom smirks, then blinks rapidly.

Damn, that was quick.

"I just don't get it. You said they found Greta, so why am I still hiding away?" It makes no sense, yet perfect sense. The danger is gone, but I would bet that a particular violet-eyed demon doesn't want the complications that having me around would bring him. God forbid he has to face his feelings. I take Dom's glass when he sways and bumps into the center island. "You okay?" I ask in mock concern.

His eyes flutter before shooting open as he tries to fight the sedative. "Camil..."

"Yes?"

His eyes lazily drag over my face. "What did you do?" His words slur, and he nearly tips over, so I guide him to the living room, where he collapses onto the couch.

"I'm sorry, Dom, but I refuse to be his prisoner."

"Cam..." His words fade, and his eyes drift shut as he gives in to the drug.

I kiss his forehead. "Thank you for watching over me, but your job is done." I cover his big body with the throw blanket, grab my go bag, and walk out of the cabin without a backward glance.

It's time to leave this world behind and, with it, the man I love.

I've already disabled the central security system and spliced in footage recorded from a few days ago— who would notice? Every day since Boian drugged me and stole me away to his Swiss cabin, every day has been the same, so it will take his team to detect that the current feed they're watching is from three days ago. Lorenzo isn't the only one with a knack for hotwiring a security system.

My inner villain wants to cackle and tap my fingers together like a Bond villain, but time is money. Speaking of which, I need to make it to a bank and withdraw some on-the-run funds before my smooth hacker job is discovered.

I tread through the ankle-deep snow and grab the old bike Dom and I found while exploring the small Swiss village just over the hill from Boian's cabin. The shopkeeper said he was just using it for a conversation starter and to get people to come inside his store, but that we could take it since the season slowed down and it was just rusting away on his stoop. I swiped it up without hesitation and asked Dom to attach a small motor so that I could ride from the cabin to the shops much faster. He agreed, but only under the understanding that he was still driving the Rover beside me while I rode.

My heart pinches, and my stomach churns at the thought of the big guy's brotherly protectiveness and how worried he will be when he wakes up and sees that I'm gone. I shake my head and focus on keeping the old motor running.

"Come on, baby. Just a little farther," I coo at the sputtering bike right before it gives out with a black puff of smoke and a sound reminiscent of an old man coughing up a lung after his tenth cigarette.

Luckily, it's only a couple of more blocks to the bank. So, with a silent thank you to the old boy, I set the bike to the side and look behind me one last time, but the cabin is nowhere in sight, swallowed up by the distance I put between me and it, and now it's time to do the same with the Roma mafia life.

Sighing, I swing my backpack over my shoulders and start walking. I'm laser-focused on my path when suddenly the hairs on the back of my neck stand on end like being outside in a lightning storm. I stop and glance in the window of a small bakery, pretending to drool over the cakes, loaves of bread, and pies sitting on display, while really, I'm searching the reflection for anything out of place or *anyone*.

When nothing jumps out at me—literally or fig-uratively—and the feeling has dissipated, I continue

on my mission to make it to the bank before any of my *famiglia* shadows are alerted.

Almost there, Camil.

4

Boian

"She's what?" I howl at my man in charge of monitoring the digital security for my place in Switzerland where I hid Camil away. I am on my way to the cabin now when he calls to inform me Camil is nowhere to be found, and he just noticed that the "live" feed is a spliced recording from days earlier.

"She's gone, Boss. Once the cameras went live again, I went back to retrieve the original feed, but someone made sure it was unusable."

I wonder who that someone is—fucking stubborn woman.

I don't bother letting him finish speaking. I hang up and call my men at the various locations of my safe house. She isn't at my cabin in the mountains where I left her or at my flat in Lucerne—the flat not even my don and best friend Emiliano knows about.

I arrive at my cabin an hour later to find Dom snoring on the couch, the doors, windows, and alarm all secured, and Camil nowhere in sight.

I stomp over to Dom's sprawled body and shove his foot off the couch. "Wake up, fucker. You have some explaining to do." He doesn't so much as flinch. Instead, he lies there sleeping like a fucking baby. My blood boils. I send the glass coffee table flying to shatter against the stone fireplace. The sound of metal on stone and shattering could wake the dead but not a sleeping Dom it seems. I'm about to start punching the asshole when my eyes catch on the crystal glass lying on the ground to the side of the couch. I pick it up to see the remnants of orange pulp suck to the sides and... "Son. Of. A. Bitch."

When I'm finally able to wake Dom's ass up to find out what the fuck happened, he takes me through his and Camil's morning. We both know what happened when he gets to the part about her offering him his morning orange juice. The little minx drugged her guard and slipped out.

Very few people know that Camilla Radu is the modern-day Marie Curie when it comes to chemistry. She typically sticks with organic mixtures—her Roma roots run deep—so it's curious that she chose a synthetic as her drug of choice. As for getting past the security system... that would be my fault. Camil has a way of talking me into teaching her shit, justifying it by saying it was for her protection. That's how she talked me into teaching her how to bypass a fairly complex security system in the off chance she was ever taken.

Idiota!

"I don't fucking get it. Why would she run?" Dom asks around another yawn.

20

"Because she's pissed that I locked her away, and now she's throwing a tantrum," I grumble and scan the perimeter cameras both here and at my flat on the off chance that she made a mistake.

"But she knows we have Greta back; therefore, you would be coming for her. Wouldn't she want to see her friend again?"

"Who knows what is going on in that head of hers?" I grouch.

"She wouldn't abandon her entire family at least, right?" The latter comes out accusatory, and I don't blame him. Dom's known Camil almost as long as Emil and I have, and he's closer to her than any other guards. In fact, if Dom weren't gay, I would have never put him as her guard. The guy is a mountain at six foot five, stacked with muscle, and a face that women literally step over each other to get to.

"I have no doubt she's keeping a close eye on all of us," I say more to myself because if I know *mia fiore* (my flower), she will be unable to stray too far from those she loves. And that's how I plan on catching the little snapdragon. She'll have to come out of hiding to check on her family, exposing herself to the beast hunting her.

My cock grows stiff at the thought of hunting her down and punishing her, branding my palm print on the soft olive skin of her ass, silencing her protest with the expensive silk tie she gave me for Christmas last year. Or maybe I'll stuff the pair of panties she snuck into the pocket of my jeans a few months back into her mouth. All good ideas and all will come to fruition once I track her down and drag her home—my home—where she belongs.

"Frankly, I don't give a shit about the why. We need to find her before she gets herself into trouble. Our enemies know who she is and won't hesitate to use her as leverage."

"Pfft, if the little pest doesn't shoot them full of arsenic first. I still can't believe she drugged me."

I smile at Dom's bewilderment. "I think it's safe to say you underestimated what Camilla Radu will do when backed into a corner."

"How pissed is Emil?" he asks with a cringe.

"Extremely, but not at you. We both know what Camil is capable of." I sigh and scratch at my beard. "However, there's one thing you don't do, and that's worry the fiancée of the most powerful man in Italy. When I find her, Camil will be lucky not to be chained to a wall in the warehouse."

"Are they postponing the wedding?" Dom asks.

"No. Greta wants to, but Emil refuses to wait any longer. They'll be married in two weeks."

"That's how we draw her out," Dom voices my thoughts. "There's no way Camil can resist crawling out of her hiding spot when she gets wind of their wedding."

"Our thoughts exactly. That's why we will 'leak' the information to the newspapers that the happy couple will marry in Olbia in two weeks. Camil is smart. She knows Emil won't risk Greta's safety by holding the wedding in an open venue. She'll know it will be held at his villa. She may not come on the property, but she'll be close."

Dom nods and scrubs a hand over the scruff of his jaw. "We'll get her." He turns mischievous eyes to me. "And she's going to regret running from her family."

"Yes, she will," I agree and dial Emil.

"*Sì, mio amico?*" He answers with a smile in his tone, and I hate to be the one to sabotage his happiness, but he is the don and must be informed of all matters concerning the *famiglia*.

"Camil ran. She drugged Dom, hacked the security, and slipped away. She's not at any of my other locations. Dom and I will head back to Olbia to debrief once we're sure she's not still in the area. Then I'm going after her." I leave no room for argument and appreciate it when Emil doesn't.

"Find her! I do not care what you have to do—who you have to kill. Find her." He disconnects without another word, and I turn to Dom.

"Time to hunt, my friend."

5

Camil

I know hiding out in my ancestral country is risky, but I need a place where I can blend in with the native people, and the icy winds blowing from Russia aid in keeping my identity concealed. During February in Romania, the temperature ranges between -3° and 4°C, so heavy jackets, scarves, and gloves are a necessity. Most foreign travelers visit in the summer, so prices are lower in February, and the crowds are much smaller.

Withdrawing funds and sneaking my way through Europe with a boatload of cash in my bag isn't easy but manageable. However, staying one step ahead of Boian and Emil is a constant headache. Whenever I come up with a way to remain hidden, I stop and think, *would they expect that?* If the answer is yes, then I do the opposite.

With its slightly warmer temperatures, culture, and museums to entertain me, Bucharest had been my preference. Instead, I chose to rent a cabin tucked away in the Apuseni Mountains, far from the meddling world and modern civilization.

I know the cash flow will eventually dry up, and I won't risk withdrawing more when the time comes, so I will ultimately need to get a job, which isn't a problem. Because of my love of the outdoors, I have a job as a tour guide lined up with The Apuseni Nature Park during the summer.

The days of keeping a crime lord organized so he can take over the world are in the past. The thought lifts the boulder off my shoulders, only to drop it squarely on my chest. Every morning I wake up in this new world, my heart aches and tugs at me to go back, to run back to my family, but my brain keeps me planted firmly on my path.

The heart is a deceiver. It tells me I can have it all—my family, security, and the man I love. But it's a lie. My family is the Roma mafia, and I will always be in danger if I stay. And as for the man I love... he doesn't want me. Or at least he doesn't *want* to want me, and I have too much pride to beg for scraps of affection from him.

"Good morning, Sofia," Mr. Gheata, the local produce vendor, greets me, or whom he believes me to be. Sofia Datcu, a transplant from Suceava, is an only child with no living relatives with an admiration for the great outdoors. That is the extent of people's knowledge of me in the little cabin village; most don't even know which cabin is mine.

"Good morning," I chirp and scan the row of bell peppers, tomatoes, zucchini, and other locally grown vegetables. I pluck two of each, then add oil, grated cheese, cherry tomatoes, salt, pepper, sage, thyme, and dill to my basket. I'm making Piperchi, a traditional Romanian dish my mother made when I was little. On lonely nights when I was little, I would still smell the familiar spices and hear my mother's laughter in my head. I didn't have much time with them. Still, I miss my parents and, to this day, cling to the memories I do have of them.

Like Papa carrying me on his shoulders to watch one of the many parades during the Christmas season. Mama would laugh as I cheered and squealed in delight at the colorful characters and twinkling lights.

I shake away my melancholy and finish my shopping. I place my items in the basket I tied to the old bike I bought off a street kid that needed a few lei for food. A chill runs up my spine as I hike my leg over the side—the kind that has nothing to do with the weather but instead comes with a venomous snake hidden in a bush waiting to strike—the same kind I felt back in Switzerland.

I dismount my rusty bike and kneel, pretending to check the tires when what I'm actually doing is scanning my surroundings. The world around me is covered in thick snow, blinding white and gleaming in the morning sun. All but the smudge of black in my peripheral vision. It stands tall and unmoving, hidden from any average passerby. But I'm not an average passerby. I'm trained to find the needle in a pile of needles, the chameleon camouflaged in the leaves, and this black smudge does not fit.

Standing, I right my jacket, then discreetly turn my eyes to the small alley where I saw the shadow.

But it's gone, faded back into its dark pit. "Is every-thing all right, Sofia?" Mr. Gheata asks with a lilt of concern from his shop doorway.

Plastering a smile on my face, I turn and reassure the older man. "Yes, sir. I thought my chain was tan-gled, but everything is fine."

"I wish you would allow my son to take you home. It's freezing out here."

This time a genuine smile lifts my lips. "And I wish you wouldn't worry so much. I love riding in the snow. This," I gesture around me, "is like a winter wonder-land, and I wish to enjoy it. Not zip by it in a car. Thank you, though. Have a good day."

With a sigh, Mr. Gheata finally relents and sends me on my way, but not without another worry-filled look, and this one time, I am tempted to take him up on his offer of a ride, not because of the weather but because my instincts tell me that my shadow will show its face again. The question is, will it come with eyes of violet or death? A part of me tingles at the thought of Boian chasing me, finding me, and rav-ishing me with kisses, his body, with … love. But then I remember all the times he rejected even the barest of touches from me like I am a leper. He can barely look me in the eye, and when he does, he is a thou-sand miles away, as though he can't be bothered to give me his full attention. Then there was the night Greta and Emil walked into the middle of one of our many arguments.

"So, how's the hunt going?" I asked.

"You will need to be more specific. We are hunting for many things," Boian drawled and kept his eyes on his phone, where he typed out text after text.

"The Rome trader," I clarified, and that got his attention.

"You know about the slave trade going on in Rome?"

I rolled my eyes and sipped from my wine. I wasn't a wine drinker, but I was health conscious enough to know to have a glass of red wine each night. "What exactly do you think I do for the *famiglia*, Boian? Get dressed up and parade around with a stack of blank papers to look like I'm doing something?" I accused, and that asshole had the nerve to shrug. "Well, I don't. I know every contract out on each person that's crossed us. I know where all the bodies are hidden and the money."

"You shouldn't know any of that. You should have stayed in school and––"

"Become a what? A nurse, a teacher, or are those even too above my competency level?"

Boian sighed and finally dropped his phone to the table and looked at me, and I would be lying if I said those violet eyes of his didn't make a swarm of doves take flight in my stomach.

"Your competency isn't the issue."

"Then what is?" I folded my arms over my chest to hide the fact that it was becoming more and more difficult to breathe the longer he stared into my eyes.

"Your naivete," he returned and sipped his vodka.

"Naivete!" I screeched. "I am not naïve."

He chuckled. "Tell that to the girl who followed me around like a lost puppy since she was five years old." He downed the rest of his drink while I steamed in my seat. "Jesus, you think you would grow out of it, but the moment I returned from the army, you were right at my heels again. And now you speak as though being privy to the Calvano Roma mafia's secrets is a testament to how fucking smart you are when really, you're ignorant and sheltered. Like I said— naïve."

I was shaking in my chair as I processed his harsh words. The man had no idea what I had been through with the fucking Roma *famiglia*. He didn't know how I found the worst jobs around the house just to stay out of the way of Idris and his men because I grew breasts the first summer after he and Emil left for the service. He didn't know I was forced to watch every execution Idris deemed necessary, then made to clean up their brain matter from the concrete outside his home. He didn't know because he wasn't there!

I can't remember another time I have ever been that enraged.

Because you've never been so hurt by the man you love.

My fist clenched the stem of my wine glass, and I spoke through clenched teeth. "Fuck you, Boian Greco. You don't know shit about what I have and have not seen or done. As for following you around like a lost puppy, consider that phase over. Continue to act as though I'm not even here."

"Believe me, I would love nothing more, but as you pointed out, you know all the Calvano secrets and, therefore, must be protected."

"Perhaps, but it doesn't have to be you. Congratulations, Boian. I relieve you of your family duty of protecting the ignorant, naïve little shut-in. You are not my guard nor my——"

"*Silenziosa,*" Boian grumbled when Greta and Emil walked into the dining room, their faces flushed and their smiles absolutely scandalous.

Greta's eyes narrowed on Boian, and her lips parted in a snarl, then closed before Emil escorted her to her chair, pulling it out for her like a gentleman.

"Thank you for waiting." Greta smiled brightly at me, and I nodded and served myself a healthy portion of the aperitivo. As though my mind wasn't wild with all the ways I could dismember the man beside me, at the same time, my heart slowly crumbled under his cruel words. The four of us carried on two con-versations——the men about work while Greta and I discussed the new meditation techniques I'd learned and how Alto had taken over Rooster's training.

It was all so domestic. If anyone off the streets had walked in right then, they would have thought we were just a typical family having dinner together and enjoying each other's company. They wouldn't see the imprisoned Conti girl that had fallen for her captor across the table from me or the two sitting side by side—yet so far away.

6

Boian

S he isn't in Italy––not that I expect her to be. Even if I don't have our men searching the entire country, I know Camil is smart enough to leave Italy.

Dom and I fly back to Olbia when we are certain she isn't still in Switzerland. By the time we return, Lorenzo is finally able to download the video of her withdrawing thirty-thousand euros from her account. Like the intuitive woman she is, she looks at the camera and mouths the words "I'm sorry," then walks away, and that is the last time we see Camil. It seems my flower paid attention when I taught her how to stay off the grid in case anything happened to Emil or me, and she needed to hide from our enemies. I just never thought she would use it against her own family.

Regardless, I will find her, and when I do, she will never be allowed out of my sight again because I plan to tie her to me in every way possible. That's if Greta will stop busting my balls.

"Seriously, Boian? What the hell are you thinking?" Greta grouses from Emil's office sofa.

"I'm thinking about what's best for Camil. She——"

"Bullshit! You're pulling one of those, 'Me man, you woman. You obey caveman' moves. Even when you find Camil, she's not going to care about some signature on a contract because she's going to be too busy tearing your balls off——"

"*Perla!*" Emil's stern scolding halts Greta's verbal tirade, but not the daggers she throws my way. "Give Boian and me a minute."

Greta swings her gaze to her fiancé. "You're kicking me out? Why, so you two can dictate *another* woman's future?" I wince internally at her harsh reminder to her fiancé of how not too long ago, he had her kidnapped and locked away. I swear, the woman has bigger balls than any man in the Calvano organization. Then again, she has the undying love and devotion of the don. Emil would never lay a violent hand on her. Though, Emil's menacing silence would make anyone think otherwise. Staring stoically at his soon-to-be wife, he quietly relays his disapproval of her disrespect.

Only when Greta begins to fidget in her seat does he finally speak. "While your voice will always be heard, *mia perla,* I will have the last say in all matters that involve the *famiglia.* Camil has known since she was a child that she will marry someone within the organization." Greta goes to argue, but Emil silences her with a lift of his hand. "Tell me, would you rather I barter her hand in marriage for an alliance? Or to a politician for more power? Or would you prefer her to marry someone who will treat her well and always put her welfare above all else?"

With a slump of her shoulders, Greta releases a dejected sigh and answers her fiancé. "I prefer she marries someone that actually *loves* her." She side-eyes me and continues. "But I get what you're saying." She stands and approaches Emil with a look of apology. She leans into his ear and whispers something that has his hands fisting and his jaw clenching.

"I will collect tonight. Be ready." He stands abruptly, causing Greta to stumble back a step, but Emil catches her with a hand around her throat.

He whispers something back to her, and her throat bobs with a heavy swallow beneath his hand before she nods and says, "*Sí,* Don Calvano." And then exits his office.

The entire exchange between the couple pulls at something inside my chest, eliciting a deep ache that pulses through my fossilized heart and lights a fire in my belly. I may never say the words Camil wants to hear, but I can show her. I need to find *mia fiore,* and it needs to be now.

"She's right, you know," Emil says once Greta vacates his office. "Camil will tear your balls off when she sees this." He lifts the marriage contract I had our lawyer draw up.

"I'm aware," I say with a sigh. "But once we're married, my name will give her the protection of the family."

"Camil will have our protection regardless of her marital status, but I understand your reasoning. What I don't understand is, why now? Why not five years ago? Why not the day you got home from the service?" My best friend and don probes, and I don't have to think hard to come up with my reason.

"I was giving her time to find..." I swallow the tightness in my throat at what I was about to say, the thought leaving a sour taste in my mouth and the need to kill screaming through my veins.

"To find?" Emil prompts.

"A good man," I finish, then walk out of his office to Emil's words trailing behind me.

"There are no good men in our world."

He's right, but any other man would be better than me. Yes, I will protect Camil with my life, but she deserves a man with a soul, and I sold mine the minute I signed up to be a paid mercenary years ago, not for the money but for the high. Now I'm paying the price because no amount of danger or living on the edge of life and death will pardon me from the demons scratching at the surface of my mind.

The only time I ever felt the slightest relief from my demons was on that beach the day I returned home when Camil was in my arms, her lips pressed to mine. We were the only two people in the world, and for the first time in my life, I saw past the blood, torn apart bodies, and screams of battle. I wasn't the man who killed an innocent woman and her children. I was just a man kissing the woman he couldn't stop thinking about—showing her with his kiss what he couldn't say with his words.

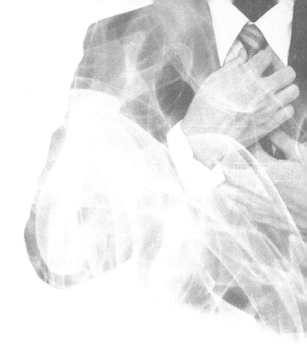

7

The Past
Boian

"Welcome home, Bo." Camil's smooth voice sent a sensual shiver down my spine and straight to my cock.

I turned from the conversation with the head of foreign affairs and *mio Dio*, I was not prepared for the full impact of *mia fiore* standing in front of me in a tight black bandage dress with a plunging neckline with sheer, delicate lace at her neck. The awkward young girl with long lanky arms and legs, and eyes, and lips that seemed too big for her face was long gone, replaced by a woman with the face of an angel and the body of a siren.

"Camil," I answered like an *idiota*.

"That's all? No, 'Hey, kid, I missed you' or something remotely close to affectionate for the girl you grew up with?"

She was teasing me, but her taunt held a shadow of vulnerability, as did her deep storm-cloud-colored eyes. I wanted to tell her she was the only person I looked forward to seeing after the shit I'd seen and done. But there was no room for pussy emotions like that in the Roma mafia.

So, I ignored her question and asked my own. "How's school?" I tucked my hands in my pockets to keep myself from reaching out to her and crushing her to me for a bruising kiss.

She sighed, "I quit," and curled a long ebony lock around her finger, and I wondered how many times I could wrap her hair around my fist before plunging my cock deep into her warm pussy. "It seemed tedious when I was already handling the administrative duties in the *famiglia* since before you two left, and I suppose Idris didn't see a reason to change that fact while you were gone." A shadow crossed over her face when she mentioned the elder Calvano before she cast it away with a bright smile, but it was too late. I'd already seen it, and not for the first time, I wanted to question her about what happened the night she called Emiliano, begging him to come and get her, and only stopped myself from asking because of Emiliano's order to drop the subject.

"And Emil is okay with you not finishing school?" I asked instead.

She rolled her eyes and waved away my words like they were absurd. "Pfft. He would be a hypocrite if he did. You both had a full ride to university but chose the armed forces instead. Besides," she shrugged, "on-the-job training is the best education."

She wasn't wrong. Emil and I didn't take our full ride, instead choosing to learn on the battlefield. Yes, we were hypocrites for being disappointed in her for not attending university, but it didn't stop me from wishing she stayed in school if only to find a life outside our world. Yes, she was destined to marry a member of the *famiglia*––a thought that haunted me every waking moment––but at least during her time in school, she could find a semblance of normalcy, if only for a little while.

"You want to go for a walk?" Camil asked and chewed on her bottom lip, her tell that she was nervous and fucking Viagra to my already aching cock.

I should have said no. "Sure."

We took the short garden path down to the beach, where the sun had dipped below the horizon, casting a halo of pinks, purples, and oranges across the Italian sky. The breeze carried the salty taste of the Tyrrhenian Sea, and the sound of waves lapping against the sand was a welcome reprieve from the violent screams and gunfire that constantly played in my head.

"I love it here," Camil whispered beside me, her gray eyes locked on the sunset. "Emil's penthouse in Rome is lovely, but Rome is too busy. For the longest time, I thought the chaotic life of Rome was what I wanted. But now..."

"Now?"

She shrugged again. "I don't know. I guess now I see myself in a place like this. Calm, tranquil. I mean, I'm not stupid. I know my life is with the *famiglia* and that I will marry a man of Emil's choosing one day." She side-eyed me at the latter, and my stomach dropped to my feet, and rage boiled my blood at the thought of any man touching *mia fiore.* "So, there will always be a bit of chaos in my life. Still, it would be nice to come home to a husband and children, grab a blanket, and sit on the beach all day as a family."

Her words were like a punch to the gut because they only validated that I was not the man for her. Even if I took Camil as my wife, children were not in my future. There was no way in hell I was bringing a child into this world to be raised by a man with enough blood on his hands that Lady McBeth would gasp in horror.

We were far away enough from the party that the music playing was barely a hum on the wind. Camil stopped, stooped to pluck a sea daffodil from the sand, and handed it to me. "A welcome home present." She smiled, and all rational thought, every reason not to touch, kiss her, to take her, flew out the window with that smile.

In one long stride, I was in front of her, pulling her to me, cold stone against warm softness. With my hands on her cheeks and the beast scratching at its bars, I crashed my lips down on hers. Her mouth opened with a gasp before she moaned against my lips, the sound driving my cock against my zipper and my hands to search out her petal-soft skin. Her fingers dove into my hair, and she pressed her soft breasts harder into my chest.

"Camil," I breathed her name like a prayer, lifted her from her feet, and pressed her back against one of the dozen boulders on the secluded beach.

Camil wrapped her legs around my waist, but not even the sound of the fabric of her dress tearing stopped her from plunging her tongue into my mouth as we devoured each other. I ground my denim-clad cock against her lace-covered pussy. Camil purred in my arms when my hands kneaded the soft globes of her ass, her dress now hitched above her waist. The fingers of one hand traced the trim of her panties until I came to the soft lips of her pussy, and I groaned when I found her hot and dripping.

"You're soaked, *fiore*," I spoke around her frenzied kiss. "Tell me. Is all that sweet nectar for me?"

"*Sí*, yes. Oh God, Bo, I've dreamt of this. Your hands on me, your mouth..." She punctuated her words with a nip to my bottom lip, eliciting a growl from my chest.

"Me too, *mia fiore*. You have no idea," I said against her lips, then groaned when she ground her pussy against my hand, still stroking her lips.

"Please, Boian. Make me come. Please, please––" Her words turned to gasps when I plunged a finger inside her weeping pussy, and fuck, she was tight.

Too tight. Virginal...

Fuck! What was I doing? Camil wasn't mine to take, nor was her virginity. Emil wasn't so old-fashioned that he thought the woman should be a virgin upon marriage. Still, I had no right to take this from her.

Like the frigid waves of the sea in December, my body went cold, and my movements stilled.

"Please don't stop." Camil's words ghosted over my lips, and as quickly but as carefully as possible, I dropped her legs back to the sand and righted her dress, now torn to mid-thigh at the seam.

I stepped back and ran shaky hands through my hair, where I gripped the short strands painfully and roared into the night sky. "FUCK!"

"Bo?" Camil's timid voice pulled at the dead organ in my chest. I gathered the last of my control and schooled my features before I turned to her, only to be swallowed up by self-loathing at the tears that sparkled in the moonlight as they fell from her stormy gray eyes. "What... What happened? Why––"

"This will not happen again. You're not mine to take, Camil," I gritted.

"But I can be. I'm your *fiore*, remember? We obviously feel something for each other..." She trailed off, so much hope in her eyes, and I knew what I must do.

"You mean that?" I pointed to the boulder I ravished her against. "That was lust, Camil, and I would have fucked you if you weren't a fucking *virgin*." I spat the word like a curse. "But you are a virgin and must remain intact for the man you marry."

"Intact?" she snarled, and the fiery Roma woman in her emerged. Her cheeks flushed an angry crimson, her eyes narrowed, and her accent thickened as she spoke. "Fuck you, Boian Greco! I'm not a little girl anymore, and I don't play games. You don't think I know what you're doing? You're pushing me away, and you know what? One day you'll push too far, and I'll be gone––at least to you. Is that what you want?" she finished on a sob.

And being the cruel bastard I was, I said, "That's exactly what I want," then walked away, leaving my dead heart at her feet.

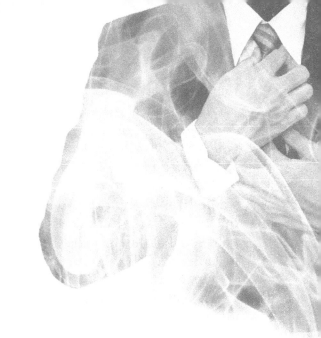

8

Present Day
Camil

The fire in the small stone fireplace radiates cozy warmth throughout the small cabin, and a contented sigh leaves my lips with a small smile. The moment is a slight reprieve from the constant nagging of my heart telling me to go home. I'm sure the feeling will dissipate as time passes, but currently, it's determined to pump as much doubt as possible through my veins.

I bring the piping hot țuica to my lips and blow a steady stream of cool breath over the surface, and even the small waves it creates reminds me of the cyan waves of the Tyherrian Sea. Growling in frustration, I discard my drink in favor of the newspaper, where I check on the weekly goings-on in the world outside my humble cabin. As soon as I unfold the paper, Emiliano and Greta's smiling faces stare back at me. The photo was taken at a charity event for trafficking survivors, and my already conflicted feelings bubble up in the form of tears, but I refuse to let them fall. That is until I read the headline:

Notorious bad boy and rumored mafia don Emiliano Calvano is set to marry his

American fiancé in two weeks.

I don't need to read the article, and even if I wanted to, I can't––not with the dagger sticking out of my back. I know it's unreasonable to feel betrayed that they would go on with the wedding in my absence. Still, it doesn't stop the sting.

We all have to move on, Camil.

I fold the paper and lay it on the side table when a thought occurs to me—one that slaps me in the face like a dueling glove. Emiliano smiling like a buffoon is out of the ordinary, but allowing himself––and, more importantly, Greta––to be openly photographed is absurd. It just doesn't happen. So why now?

A sarcastic smile stretches my lips. *Well played, Calvano. Or was it Boian's idea?* Either way, I'm not falling for their tricks––no matter how much I long to be there to watch my friends say their vows to each other. That's precisely what they expect me to do, and I would be nabbed by one of the soldiers the moment my foot hit the Olbia city limits.

Leaning my head back with a sigh, I let the vision of Greta walking down the aisle in her simple white wedding dress play out behind my closed eyelids. She would be a light amongst all the darkness in our world and a fierce queen for her king. We would laugh as we tried to swallow the champagne we hated. Boian would ask me to dance and touch me tenderly as he guided me effortlessly around the dance floor. The world around us would disappear, and we would finally say the words I have dreamt about him saying for years. *"Ti amo, mia fiore."* *I love you, my flower,* and we would make love all night to the sound of the sea crashing against the sand...

Bolting upright, I shake the images from my head because dreaming of a fairy tale life is useless and only makes me weak.

Suddenly, there's a heavy knock at the cabin door. My shoulders instantly stiffen, and my heart leaps to my throat. I snatch the rifle from beneath the sofa and approach cautiously before peeking out the small window to the side of the door. A man dressed in black, literally from head to toe, stands there, gloved hands folded in front of him, back ramrod straight, and despite the thick black scarf blocking the view of his face, I would know that military posture anywhere.

"Shit. Shit, shit, shit," I whisper growl.

"Camil!" Boian's fist rattles the door on its hinges. "I know you're in there."

I whisper another curse, turning to grab my go-bag as silently as possible when the door suddenly splinters and the door jamb cracks. I hold back a startled squeak, lay the rifle down, and then bolt for the hallway to the attic access. I pull down the stairs, then sprint up them like a rabid dog is on my heels because one may very well be. Just as I'm shutting the door and latching it, I hear the front door hit the wall, then heavy booted steps. I tip-toe like a cartoon character over the creaky attic floorboards to the small round window, and not for the first time, I thank God I kept up with my yoga. Otherwise, there is no way my ass could fit through this window. I oiled the hinges not too long ago, so when I swing it open, it doesn't make a peep. I gently place my go-bag on the snow-covered tile roof below, then swing one leg out as the attic ladder squeaks and light pours in from the open door. When both feet are ankle-deep in snow, I grab my bag and make my way down the rooftop to the trellis I tested the same day I oiled the window's hinges. I scramble down the trellis, barely catching myself when my foot slips on one of the foot holes. As soon as I'm safe on the ground, I bolt for the mountain base, where a thick forest stands tall, waiting for me to hide in its wild depths—all part of my escape plan. If it wasn't Boian coming for me, then an enemy of the family could, so I slept in the freezing forest for two days to ensure I could survive. It was hell on earth, but I made it.

"Damn it, Camil!" Boian shouts from the tiny attic window, and I laugh as I peek over my shoulder to see his head sticking out of the window, his broad shoulders keeping him from coming after me.

"Nice try, Bo!" I shout back and flip him the finger, but my victory is short-lived when an arm goes around my neck, and a hard chest hits my back.

"My apologies, Camil," Dom's voice holds no genuine apology as he tightens the triangle hold on my neck. Before my vision goes fuzzy and the world goes black, Boian's violet eyes, muddied with contempt, are the last things I see.

9

Boian

Romania. That's where my flower fled after withdrawing thirty thousand euros from her account. Then she vanished––or at least she thought she did. Camil is slick, I'll give her that, but she forgot that I'm the one who taught her everything she knows, and no matter how indifferent I was to her over the years, I was secretly watching her, protecting her... craving her. She may believe she's a nobody in our world, but she's more valuable than all the riches our family brings to the table––clean or not. She is priceless.

She's limp in my arms as I carry her back to the small cabin and lay her on the queen bed in her room. For seconds, minutes—who the hell knows how long—I stand at her bedside and stare down at my flower. She's tiny compared to my towering height. With a face and body of a goddess, she is every man's wet dream. Her long ebony mane feathers around her head, her unusual storm cloud gray eyes hidden beneath eyelids with naturally full dark lashes, and her lips that seem to have a permanent pout twitch as she starts to stir.

Camil groans and brings her gloved hand to her forehead before her lashes flutter and her eyes open, and the moment they do, they lock on me, and she smiles sweetly. And damn if that smile doesn't nearly bring me to my knees. But as quickly as the smile comes, it's gone when she recalls what happened just moments before. And like the spitfire she is, Camil does a side roll off the bed like a cheesy action hero, then stands, legs apart, fists up, and shoulders tucked just like I taught her.

I stare at her emotionlessly when I'm anything but. My heart begins to race, my palms sweat, and my face flushes with the need to tackle her to the bed and finally dip my cock in her sweetness. But that will have to wait. And *it will happen* because fuck it. I'm done denying myself. Camil is mine, and I'm done watching her date losers not worth the mud on her boots. I'm not worthy of her either, but I'm selfish enough not to give a shit.

I cross my arms over my chest, releasing an irritated sigh. "Really, Camil? You want to fight me physically? How well do you think that will go down?"

"What? You don't think you taught me well enough, Bo?" She cracks her neck, and I would laugh if I weren't so fucking hard for her right now.

"Apparently not. Dom was able to incapacitate you without a fight." This time I do smirk.

Camil's gray eyes narrow on me. "He caught me off guard." I open my mouth to mock that she shouldn't have been caught off guard in the first place, but she continues with her excuses. "*And* when I heard it was Dom, I didn't fight because I didn't want to hurt him." Her eyes drop in regret before they lift and steel once again.

"Right. You prefer to drug the poor guy and leave him to wake up scared shitless when he sees the woman he considers a sister *gone*." This time when her eyes drop, guilt shadows their silver glow. And being the asshole I am, I take advantage of her brief moment of vulnerability. Quick as a pouncing lion, I jump over the bed and barrel into her. She lets out an audible squeal when my chest hits hers, and my hands grip her ass, lifting her and dropping her on the bed before laying atop her, my chest pressed firmly to hers. Her jacket acts as a barrier, but it doesn't stop my skin from sizzling and my dick from straining painfully against the zipper of my jeans. Or my hips from swaying and pressing against hers, letting her feel what she does to me, and by the little gasp she releases, I know she's gotten the message.

I lean in to bring my nose to hers and watch her pupils dilate. Her tongue wets a path across her soft velvet lips, and I nearly groan with the image of those lips stretched to the max around my cock as I skull fuck my little flower. I press my erection against the seam of her pants and smirk when she gasps, and her dark lashes flutter closed. "Here's how things are going to go, my flower."

Her eyes open and burn like melted steel. "Don't call me that!" she grumbles like a petulant child, but I ignore her, choosing to run the tip of my nose over hers and revel in the small whimper that leaves her lips.

"We will stay right here until I can trust you won't run off again. I, Lorenzo, or Dom will watch you every second of the day." She shakes her and goes to argue, but I silence her with a firm hand over her mouth. "I'm not done. While here, you will obey me. I will control everything you do, and you will work to please me. Only when I feel you're ready will you be welcomed home," I finish with a growl because though I'm gagging to fuck her, I'm still pissed at her betrayal.

"Let me get this straight. You want me to jump when you say jump, sit when you say sit, say when I eat, sleep, and whatever the hell else?"

I smile against her cheek, causing my whiskers to rub against her soft skin. "That is exactly what you will be doing. Very good, *my flower,*" I mock and groan against her skin when she bucks beneath me, then gasps when I grind my stiff cock against the seam of her pants.

"I'm not your fucking dog, Bo," she breathes, then moans when I swivel my hips and thrust against her sex.

"You're right. You're not my dog," I agree with another swivel of my hips, "but you are *mine,* Camil Radu." I finish with a hard thrust and watch her eyes roll back in her head and her lips quiver as she comes. She fucking comes. I can't help my surprise. Then again, if I had less self-control, I would be right there with her. As it is, I rise from the bed and walk to the bedroom door, only stopping long enough to throw over my shoulder, "Get some rest, Camil. Your training begins bright and early," then slam the door before the small glass vase she throws at me hits its target. Her colorful curses breach the thin wood door, and I can't help but smile and shake my head.

I call Camil *mia fiore*, but she isn't some dainty tulip or daisy. No, Camil Radu is an Oleander.

Beautiful, but lethal.

10

Camil

I came. I fucking came just by Boian dry-humping me. But in my defense, I never denied that I found the man unbelievably attractive. A beast among men but a sexy as hell beast, and with those words on his lips, *You're mine, Camil Radu,* and his hard length hitting my clit just right, I can't be mad at myself for coming like a teenage girl exploring her sexuality for the first time. No, I am furious that no matter how he ignored me, denied me, and lied, I couldn't seem to hate Boian Greco.

It's been that way since that day at Emil's house when I played while my mother was at the doctor and my father was meeting with Idris. Boian picked up my tiny five-year-old body and carried me to Gillie—Emiliano's mother—for her to patch me up after I fell from twirling in circles like a loon and scraped my knee. I knew I liked the orphan boy with shaggy black hair and weird eyes. He stood beside me quietly while she applied the antiseptic, and when I whimpered at the sting, he took my hand and said, "Be brave little flower. Pain only lasts a little while." My young heart pitter-pattered in my chest for the weird-eyed boy. I couldn't stop smiling for the rest of the day as I ran around telling everyone who would listen how Bo saved my life. It was so long ago, but the memory is still fresh in my mind.

But soon, that boy was forced to become a man well before he should have when Emil and Boian were subjected to Idris's cruelty. All three of us would see the grizzly reality of living in our world when Emil's mother was dropped off at our doorstep, beaten and bloodied, her eyes wide open, staring off into the endless pit of death.

The Vasiles paid for her brutal death. Of course, it wasn't until recently that we found out that Idris himself had killed her after he caught onto her plan to flee with Emil and right into her lover's arms.

Idris's crimes against Gillie weren't a surprise. For years, I watched him beat his son and Boian bloody with the reasoning that he was preparing them for life in the Calvano Roma mafia. In reality, it was because he knew, even at a young age, that the boys were stronger, smarter, and more capable of leading the family.

We were each other's anchors. I tended to their bruises and lacerations and learned how to sew up a knife wound at an early age. I emotionlessly helped reset bones and dislocated shoulders before sobbing into my pillow each night. They tried to shield me from the worst, and I believe if it wasn't for them, I would have been raped by more than one of Idris's men. We were a team ... until we weren't.

They left to serve their country... They left me. I knew how selfish I sounded. I should have told them how proud I was of them, but I didn't... I couldn't. All I could do was stare at them in quiet rage, then turn my back and walk away as they left for basic training, the bitter taste of betrayal coating my tongue. The tears of abandonment stung my eyes, and the fear of losing them shackled my heart with thorny vines. I was a teenage girl stuck in a house full of deviants without my protectors. I tried to stay to myself and out of Idris's way, working silently with the rest of the help, terrified to even look at the man. Still, it didn't stop Idris from setting up a deal to sell me to a prince known for his brutal treatment of his slave girls. I left the elder Calvano's home the next day and refused to set foot in it again.

But that was all in the past. Idris is dead, Emil and Boian have banned sex trafficking in the Calvano territory, and anyone who dares to oppose them will meet a brutal end. The here and now is what has me captured because as I lay deathly still on the lumpy mattress, Boian's words from moments before echo in my head. *Get some rest, Camil. Your training begins bright and early.* What the hell does that mean? Training? I kept up with my martial arts and weapons training back in Italy but haven't thought much about it since I snuck away to my little cabin. My main focus was staying hidden and my escape if it ever came to that—the latter needs some work.

Curiosity has me springing from the bed, the old brass frame squeaking loudly. I swing the door wide and run into a brick wall of Dom's chest. "Ow," I grumble and grab my nose to check for blood. "What the hell are you made of, Dom? Cinder blocks?" I expect to see Dom's trademark smirk when I look up, only to find narrowed eyes and a puckered brow.

"Do you need something, Camilla?" *Camilla? He's definitely pissed at me.*

"Yes. I need you to move so I can speak to Bo." I go to move around him, but he moves with me, and when I try again, he moves fluidly with me like we're stuck in some bizarre dance. Stomping my foot like a petulant child, I glare at the mountain in my path. "Move, Dom. I'm not playing games. I want to speak to him."

Dom's eyes turn lethal and laser-focused on mine when he leans into my face and growls, "Were you playing back in Switzerland when you drugged me?" I wince at his words but know better than to answer as he continues. "When you let me wake up terrified that the woman I consider a sister was gone and possibly in danger? Tell me, Camilla, were you playing then?"

Tears sting the back of my eyes, and guilt claws at my throat so much that I have to clear it before answering. "Dom, I'm sorry, but––"

"No." That word slices between us like a knife's blade. "I don't want to hear any half-assed apologies. I swore to protect you, and you not only scared the shit out of me, but you made me look like a fool."

53

"I know," I whisper dejectedly and rub at the ache in my chest where the guilt eats away from the inside out. "You're right, Dom. What I did was wrong, no matter my reasoning. You're family, and family doesn't do that to each other. I'm sorry."

To my joy, Dom drops his shoulders with a heavy sigh, and a smile reaches his lips. "You're forgiven, little bit." He engulfs me in a tight hug that pushes a grunt from my chest as he purposely crushes me to his chest.

"Okay, okay, you big oaf," I choke and push off his chest, and with a husky laugh, he releases me but doesn't move from his spot. "Enough of the love fest. Now, move so I can give the brute in the other room a piece of my mind." I chuckle and go to move around him again, but to my utter frustration, he moves with me again. "Okay, what's going on, Dom? I thought you forgave me."

His eyes are soft with a slight glimmer of mischief playing in their dark depths. "I have forgiven you, but the boss hasn't. He doesn't trust you, so you're to stay here until he comes to get you in the morning."

My mouth drops so suddenly that I'm surprised it doesn't come unhinged. "WHAT!" I wail, causing Dom to grimace at my sudden outburst. "Are you kidding me? I am not one of his enemies he can imprison and torture!"

Dom shrugs, and my temper flares. "You get his ass in here right now, Dom, or I swear I will claw your eyes out." My fists shake at my side, and I become lightheaded with the copious amount of adrenaline sprinting through my veins.

Dom curses in Romanian and then calls for Boian. My breath escapes in heavy pants, sweat dots my hairline, and my cheeks feel on fire as the warm flush of rage washes over me while I wait for the bastard to show his face.

A moment later, the man of my dreams, and now my nightmares, takes Dom's place as my roadblock. "You requested my presence, my flower?" he purrs with an up-tick of one side of his lips.

"You can fuck off with the '*my flower*' crap! You are not keeping me locked up like some disobedient child!" I seethe.

The smirk drops from his lips. "Then perhaps you shouldn't have acted like a child who didn't get their way," he growls in my face.

"Fuck you, Boian Greco," I return with my own growl.

Neither one of us blinks as we stare daggers at one another for seconds, minutes. Then as though our little spat never happened, the smirk from before returns to Boian's face——only this time, it morphs into a full panty-melting smile. My heart jumps to my throat, and my mouth waters as a shiver of desire races along my skin.

"We'll see, my flower." He runs a calloused finger over my collarbone and up to my lips, where he grazes the soft skin, and it takes all my self-control not to close my lips around the rough digit. "If you're good."

"If... If I'm good—what?" I ask breathlessly, but if Boian notices my wanton state, he's too enamored by my lips to say.

When his eyes lift to mine, I gasp at the flames of desire burning in their violet depths. "Then maybe I'll let you fuck me," he finishes, then turns on his heels and walks away as though he didn't just implode my entire world.

I stand wide-eyed, with my mouth gaping at his words. Did I hear him right? Besides the night of his welcome home party, Boian hasn't so much as looked at me with anything but annoyance.

Still stunned, I force my feet to move. "Let me... I don't... What?" Since when have I become a babbling idiot?

Boian turns back with a smirk. "Cat got your tongue, Camil?"

"No!" I burst. "There will be none of *that*, Boian Greco."

"None of what, flower? You will need to be more specific." His smile is a roguish tip of his lips, reminding me of the rare moments he would let himself laugh when we were kids.

"You know what."

He puckers his lips to one side and rubs at his beard in mock contemplation. "I'm afraid I don't."

"Fucking! There will be none of that."

Boian's eyes turn a deadly shade of purple, and his cheeks flush with desire. His hard chest rises and falls with each heavy breath, and when he takes a long, swaggering stride toward me, I can feel my panties dampen with my arousal—the man's effect on me is mind-bending. Even now, while he commands me like a disobedient pet, I want him deep inside me, touching me, kissing me, devouring me.

"Why is that, Camil? I know you want me. You want what only I can give you." His eyes slide the length of my body, his tongue licking his kissable lips before he snags the bottom one with his teeth and holy mother of God, I've never seen anything more erotic, sexier, or infuriating than this man with that look of hunger on his face.

I swallow around the need to drop to my knees and take him into my mouth to worship at his altar. "You think I want you when you're ordering me around like a pet, controlling my every move?" I scoff and cross my arms over my chest to hide the strained peaks of my nipples.

"I think that's exactly what you want." He pulls me closer, his face close enough now that I can feel his warm minty breath against my face. "I think you've been fighting your entire life, putting on a strong front."

"It's not a front," I grizzle.

"And you like the idea of someone taking control," he continues as though I never spoke. "Someone to lift the burden of decision off your shoulders. And Camil," suddenly, his hand fists my hair, and his lips brush mine when he speaks again, "I think you want that someone to be me."

My heart bangs against my chest with such force that each breath is a gasp, and my body quivers under Boian's dominant hold. *My God, can he be right?* I would be lying if I said the thought of letting go didn't give me a slight sense of peace. No, that's not possible. As much as I love my family, I have to be able to depend on myself. Otherwise, I'm going to

crumble when they leave again, and I will be left with an empty shell.

Placing a trembling hand on his chest, the battle between pulling him closer and pushing him away makes my chest pinch and my tummy flutter. Ultimately, I decide it's distance that I need. I steel my spine and stare stoically into his eyes. "Let go of me. You have nothing I want, Boian Greco."

It's a lie, and the bastard knows it. He runs the tip of his nose across mine and smiles. "Liar." Then walks out the door.

11

Boian

I have to get out of this cabin. The longer I stand there with her body pressed to mine, the more her scent of jasmine and something uniquely Camil sends my thoughts imagining all the deviant things I could do to her body. Even now, standing in the small, open living room of the cabin, the walls start to close in on me, knowing she's in the other room seething, a ticking bomb ready to explode and take out every person in the vicinity. Call me a masochist, but I find Camil's rage sexy as fuck. Her cheeks flush with crimson, her tiny breaths making her breasts rise and fall in quick succession, and those gray eyes turn nearly black with fury. Camil has a knack for keeping her emotions in check, much like the hardened men she grew up around. But with me, all that control goes out the window—a fact that will come in handy while I teach her a lesson about running off and putting herself at risk. And ultimately, when I inform her of our upcoming nuptials. Fuck. Just thinking about the fight that will ensue makes my dick hard as stone.

I swing open the front door, leaving my heavy coat on the hook by the door, and exit into the frigid Romanian air. *Home.* I was only a boy when my father moved us to Italy. My mother had been dead for less than a year, and my father couldn't wait to get the hell out of Romania. My mother country is where my parents met, fell in love, and eventually married and started a family, but as time passed, my father began to despise my mother for refusing to leave her home. The honeymoon quickly faded as my father's dreams of going to Italy to make his mark became more important than his wife's happiness.

And how did my father plan to make his mark? Who the hell knows, but the moment we stepped onto Italian soil, my father became a different person. A drunkard, the town idiot, and soon a drug mule for Emil's grandfather Fernando Calvano––until the five bags of pure Columbian cocaine dissolved inside his stomach.

Our last time together and the memory that will be seared into my mind for the rest of my life was when I watched my father convulse and foam at the mouth as the drugs were absorbed into his bloodstream. Fernando sat by and watched with a scowl, grumbling about the money my father had just cost him while I stood and watched without shedding a tear. Not because I didn't have any affection for my father but because it didn't come as a surprise, even at the tender age of eight.

The moment my father's body stopped convulsing, he was taken away. No last rights were performed, no funeral, and no further discussion other than how they would make back the money and what to do with me. None of the Calvano Roma families offered to take me in, suggesting instead to leave me on the doorstep of the many orphanages in Rome. Still, Fernando had a soft spot for his grandson, so when Emil begged his grandfather to let me stay with them, Fernando agreed—much to Idris's chagrin—and the rest is history.

The one man who gave a shit about us died, and Idris's reign dawned: a history full of beatings at the hand of Idris and his men and my demotion to drug mule as payment for my father's costly death. But where my father failed, I succeeded, and eventually, I worked my way up the ranks to be Emil's second in command.

And while Emil and I fought, maimed, and destroyed our enemies, Camil was there waiting for us to return from battle. Fierce and loyal—only for us to abandon her to fight a different battle, one we felt was necessary to keep our country strong and teach us the true art of war. Only, when Emil went home to begin taking over the Calvano empire, I stayed to quench my newfound thirst for destruction, eventually staying one mission too long.

"You're really doing this, then?" Lorenzo asks from behind me.

I don't bother turning. Instead, I keep my eyes on the horizon, watching for neighbors coming to investigate the commotion from moments ago. "Yes,"

I answer simply, and Lorenzo remains silent. Emil may be the don and has the final say, but he tasked me with commanding the Calvano soldiers, and as such, they are to follow my orders. Lorenzo may be a sadistic man when it comes to torture, but when it comes to Greta and Camil, he's a sappy fool. Not that I blame him. There's nothing more I want to do than stomp back into Camil's room, clutch her to my chest, and soothe the sting of my words. But what will that accomplish? Yes, she has us to watch over her, but a woman in the Roma mafia has to have a spine made of steel and the strength of a lioness. Camil has all of that in spades, proven by how she took care of herself while we were away in the army. Still, it doesn't stop me from wanting to relieve her of that burden. But in her present state of mind, it would be like trying to de-fang said lioness.

The thought makes me chuckle. Camil Radu. Intelligent, sassy, sexy as hell, and the biggest pain in my ass, and fuck if it doesn't turn me on.

"Dom and I will be in the cabin just over the bank if you need us," Lorenzo informs me with a note of hesitation, but when I turn to address the meta-phorical stick he has shoved up his ass, he's already walking away. At the same time, Dom steps out onto the small landing and gives a salute in goodbye.

Movement in my peripheral has me turning my eyes to the window to Camil's room, where she stands with her goddess-like beauty, a siren calling to an entranced sailor. She lifts her hand, and when I think she's going to place it on the chilled glass of the window, she surprises me when, at the last minute, she bends her arm in an L-shape, fist pointing upward with her other hand gripping the bicep of her bent arm and raising it emphatically in the traditional Italian sign to "go fuck yourself." I've pulled men's tongues from their heads with rusty pliers for less, and she knows it, yet she tells me to fuck off like she's ten feet tall and invincible. Damn, that's sexy as hell.

Not bothering to hide that I have to adjust my throbbing erection in my jeans, I smile, blow her a kiss, then watch as she pouts those petal-soft lips and stomps away from the window.

That's right, my flower. Keep trying to deny it. I love a challenge.

12

Camil

D amn that emotionless, selfish, egotistical, completely gorgeous, delicious...

Stop! Get your hussy hormones under control, Camil. You will not give in to this man... at least not until he admits his true feelings for you.

Those are the words I say to myself, but I find them harder and harder to stick to when the beast is in my presence. Even barking orders at me, Boian Greco is my weakness, and he knows it. But can I become his weakness? Can I make him want me so deeply and profoundly that he finally says and *means* those three little words? And if so, how do I do so without giving in to our sexual heat? Where do I start?

"Ugh," I groan and plop down on the bed. It's not late enough to sleep, but I find my mind and body exhausted from everything that's occurred in such a short amount of time.

I let out a jaw-stretching yawn, then let my eyelids flutter shut. The next thing I know, I'm springing upright in bed. The room is pitch black only for the bright beams of the moon. My brow is lined with sweat, and the last remnants of an orgasm skitter across my skin. I try and fail to calm my racing heart as the dream of a wild beast chasing me in the snow-laden forest lingers in my mind. His growls and heavy panting were just steps behind me before he leaped and tackled me to the icy forest floor. His face was hidden in shadows, only his violet eyes showing through the night. He trapped my hands above my head in one of his paws, then ripped my thin white nightgown from my body. I was terrified and unbelievably aroused simultaneously, and when he shoved his massive cock inside me with an animalistic grunt, my body went liquid. I moaned like a wanton heathen as he rutted inside me, the word *mine* repeated with every thrust. And when I went to call his name, it was replaced with a scream of ecstasy as the beast bit down on my neck, and an orgasm so intense it bordered on painful wracked my bones.

"Shit," I breathe and run a shaky hand through my sweat-damp hair.

"Camil?" Boian's voice sounds through the door before the nob turns, and he's standing there in nothing but a pair of thick cotton pajama pants. His chest is covered in a dark dusting of hair, his pecs and abs solid slabs of steel, with that lickable Adonis belt that disappears beneath the soft cotton of his pants where the prominent bulge of his cock takes center stage.

The lust from earlier comes racing back in full force as I eye-fuck him without shame and want to demand he gets over here and satisfy my every womanly need. Instead, all that comes out is, "Aren't you cold?" I ask around a pool of saliva that nearly dribbles down my chin when I speak.

Great! Are you literally drooling?

"You know I don't get cold, *fiore*. I'm your furnace, remember," he teases, and I can't help but smile at the memory of Emil, Boian, and I splashing each other in the icy waters of the sea. "I remember. You and Emil loved to play in the cold water. You never thought I had the balls to join you."

His abs tighten when he laughs, and his arms bulge when he crosses them over his chest and leans against the doorframe. "You proved us wrong, though. You dived right in and swore you weren't cold. Even when you shook like a leaf, and your lips turned purple." He shakes his head, still keeping his distance. Distance that I currently hate. I want him to be my furnace now as the sweat on my skin chills with the cold draft this old place invites in.

As though reading my mind, Boian's brow furrows and he approaches the bed with determination. "Get under the blanket."

He lifts the blanket, and I don't bother arguing and scurry under the handmade quilt, snuggle it up to my chin, and watch Boian light a fire in the small stone fireplace across from the bed.

"You still haven't gotten the hang of lighting a fire?" he asks with a smile painting his tone.

I shrug, even though his focus is on placing the wood in the perfect position for a roaring fire. "I can't be good at *everything*."

Once he has it to his liking, he approaches the bed again, then surprises me when he lifts the blanket and crawls in with me. He pulls on my hip until I'm on my side, facing him, hauls me to his chest, and hisses when my cold hands touch his warm skin.

"*Gesù Cristo*, woman, have you been dunking your hands in ice?" I bury my hands between the crevice of his pecs, then wrap my legs around his.

The heat from his massive muscles instantly warms my skin, and I let out a sigh of tranquility before saying, "Just call me the ice queen." My eyes droop as I melt into Boian's side, my head on his chest. "I'll let this happen tonight because I'm too exhausted to fight," I mumble while drawing circles in the hair of his chest.

Boian sighs in agitation and presses my circling hand to his chest. "Shut up and go to sleep, Camil."

I yawn and let my eyes flutter shut. "Fuck off, Bo." I breathe in his uniquely Boian scent and let my dreams take me away.

13

Boian

"You think you'll make it?" Greta asks over the *click, click,* clicking sound of her typing up her next book. She went from being a best-selling romcom author to a best-selling thriller author within months. I wasn't much of a reader, but Camil loved Greta's work. So, I decided to read one or two ... or six of her first books. At first, I felt like a pussy for reading books full of angsty characters, misunderstandings that could have been solved with a single conversation, and the sappy happily ever after. But the more I read, the more I saw the true talent it took to write these stories. And the sex scenes? Let's just say that's where Greta White shined.

"I have every intention of being there," I answer around the lip of my espresso cup.

"That's not what I asked, Boian," she throws back, and I smirk at her balls. I swear the women of this family will take over the *famiglia* if we aren't careful.

"Unfortunately, *mi regina*, I can't give you a straight yes or no answer. Camil is stubborn to a fault."

"Then let me talk to her. If she knows––"

"No," I interrupt brusquely, even though I know that if Emil heard the tone I took with his beloved *perla*, he would have my balls in a vise for the disrespect. "I can't have any interference. This is between Camil and me. She needs to come willingly and without a plan to run again as soon as the I dos are said."

Greta sighs and then agrees to drop it. "You're right. How is she doing anyway?" There's a smile in her tone. The soon-to-be Calvano queen is all too aware that I won't be going easy on my little captive, and in return, I will catch hell from my little, gray-eyed captive.

"Foaming at the mouth like a rabid dog waiting for the right moment to bite my ass."

Greta laughs so loud, I have to pull the phone from my ear. "Sounds about right. Well, tell her I said good luck," she finishes with a devious snicker, then hangs up.

Emil has his hands full with that one, and I can't help but compare the two women. Where Greta is reserved and able to slip in and out of whatever role she needs the world to believe her to be––like the queen of the Roma mafia––Camil can only be herself. She doesn't care if you see her as just a pretty face or sex on legs. In fact, she will use it to her advantage to find your weakness and rip your heart out while quoting Dante's *Inferno* word for word.

"Was that Greta?" Camil's sleep-soaked voice comes from behind me, and my cock instantly comes to attention.

"How did you know?" I ask and don't bother to hide the lustful trail my eyes take over her curvy body.

"That laugh of hers could be heard halfway around the world." She plops down in the small wood chair at the two-seater table I'm currently working at. Her hair is a wild mess of dark curls atop her head, her face is clear of makeup, and she's covered from neck to toe in a plaid pajama set. And she's never looked sexier.

I have to adjust my dick and clear my throat before I turn to her fully. "It was her. She was checking on you. At least, that's what she said. I think she wanted to make sure *I* was still in one piece," I say in good humor, but it falls flat when Camil's eyes flash with the pain of betrayal.

"So, she knows that you're keeping me captive?"

"Mhmm," I answer around another swallow of espresso.

Hurt turns to anger, and her small hands fist on the table. "After everything she went through, she's okay with you keeping me prisoner?"

I shrug. "Not really, but she understands the method behind my madness. Besides, she's pissed at you too."

"What?" she screeches. "She has a lot of nerve! She ran too!"

I nod. "True, but she thought Emil was selling women to the highest bidder and that she was next. What's your excuse?" I growl the latter. She flinches at my harsh tone, but I don't give a fuck. I want answers. Starting with this one.

Her cheeks flush, and her lips part to argue, but she realizes my intent at the last second, drops her shoulders, and leans back in her chair. "Does it matter?" She shrugs carelessly, and it's the last straw.

I have her up and flat on her back atop the small wooden table before she can utter another word. The breath gushes from between her lips, and her hands come up to guard her face before she catches herself and drops them to my forearms, but it's too late. I've seen the fear in her eyes. *Someone has hit her.* The thought has the beast inside me clawing at my chest. All thoughts of punishing her while pinned to the table vanish, and my previous question is replaced with another.

My hands land on either side of her head, and I bring my nose to hers. "Who hit you?"

Her eyes widen and sparkle with unshed tears before they narrow, her lashes flutter, and her eyes harden like granite. "No one in a very long time. Now get off of me, Bo." Fuck I love when she calls me that. It's like a shot of heroin to an addict, and warm euphoria threatens to take me over with that simple endearment.

I press my cock against the edge of the table in an attempt to calm the bastard down. "But someone did hit you." It's not a question, but she answers anyway.

"What does it matter? They're dead––"

"They? There was more than one?" Suddenly it feels like my lungs will implode beneath the implications of someone laying a violent hand on my flower, and my vision goes red at the seams.

Camil lifts her chin indignantly. "Don't worry, Bo. I fought back just like you taught me. Thanks for that, by the way. After all, you did leave me to fend for myself."

Her words hit me like a sledgehammer to the chest. I reel back and stumble over my feet before righting myself and turning from her, my chest cracking open and bleeding out with the blow of her accusation.

I hear her sit up from the table and shuffle over to where I'm standing, my hand over my mouth and a stinging pain at the back of my eyes. "Shit, Bo. I'm sorry. I didn't mean that——"

"Yes, you did!" I shout as I round on her, then curse myself and swallow the bile rising up my throat when Camil flinches. I shake my head and blink away the static that threatens to blind me. "I left men in charge of your safety. Where..." I stumble over my words. "Where were they while you were..." I can't finish my sentence, or I risk tearing the small cabin apart.

"I don't know. I... No one ever came to my aid. You really had someone watching over me?" she questions, and I stare at her, completely dumbfounded. Did she really think I would abandon her in that place without someone keeping an eye on her?

"*Gesù Cristo*, Camil. Of course, I had someone watching over you! I appointed one of our best and most trusted men to guard you. He was ordered to protect you and send me monthly reports..." My words come to a screeching halt at the sudden sadness marring Camil's beautiful face.

"Dante," she whispers.

"Yes, Dante," I confirm, trepidation crawling along my skin.

Camil nods somberly. "A couple of years after you left, Idris accused him of being a traitor. He had him tortured and eventually executed. I didn't tell you because I wanted you to focus, and I was afraid the news would distract you, putting you in harm's way. I'm sorry. I should have told you."

I take in her words, thinking back over the years during my time away, then shake my head vehemently. "No. Dante wrote to me like clockwork every month until I informed him I was coming home."

"That's not possible, Bo. I was there."

"What do you mean you were there?" I ask and dread the words that I know are about to come out of her mouth.

"Idris made all of us watch him put a bullet in Dante's skull." Camil doesn't even wince at her statement, further proving the ruthlessness of our world. The world I left her in——all alone. "Were you not curious why you never saw him again?"

My hand dives into my hair, where I grip the roots harshly, letting the sting center me as I recall the day I came home. I went to find Dante to see why he hadn't answered my texts about my arrival, only to be intercepted by Idris and told of Dante's alleged betrayal. He showed me the evidence, and I was too wrapped up in my bullshit to investigate. *Motherfucker.*

"I was told the same thing. Idris showed me the evidence of Dante's betrayal but told me he was executed only weeks before... and I fucking left it alone," I mumble the latter, sickened with myself.

A delicate hand grips my bicep, and her soft voice penetrates the self-loathing and disgust like sunshine through the fog. "Hey. It's not your fault."

While spoken in earnest tenderness, those words don't banish the disgust at my incompetence. I round on her like a cobra about to strike. "Not my fault? No, you're right, Camil. I left you to fend for yourself and at the mercy of Idris fucking Calvano." I want to resurrect the fucker only to torture and kill him over and over again. Since that's not an option, I release my rage the only way I know how. With an almighty roar, my fist lands on the wall beside me with a sickening crunch, and wood splinters beneath my knuckles with each blow I deliver to the wall.

Camil's hands pull on my forearm, and she jerks forward with each assault. "Bo, stop!" Camil shouts, but I stop only when bloody fist prints paint the wall, not because of her pleading but because it's not enough.

I stomp into the kitchen and flip over the small dining table. It spirals until it lands hard against the refrigerator, but I'm not done. The copper pot on the stove flies through the window, letting in a blast of icy wind. It's still not enough, and I'm unsure when it will be because the fuse is lit. I swing around and head toward my next victim, the small sofa in the middle of the living room, when Camil jumps on my back, her warm body blanketing me. Her petite but toned legs wrap around my waist, and her arms, covered in ugly plaid, circle my neck.

"Please, Bo," she whispers against my ear, and instantly, my skin goes from scorching with rage to warm like a summer day in Tuscany. "Breathe, and come back to me, Bo," she instructs, and as though it can't help but submit to her soft command, my breathing evens out and begins to mimic hers against my back. I'm not sure why I'm surprised at how my body listens and obeys my flower's command because Camil is the air I breathe.

We breathe as one, and the veil of fury slowly lifts from my eyes. I blink away the sweat dripping over my lashes, then turn my head to where her lips rest next to my ear. Her silver eyes search violet ones before they drop to my lips, and she brings hers closer until our lips brush against one another, and my body heats for an entirely different reason. Her eyes lift back to mine before she leans into me fully and presses her lips to mine, and like an ember to a pool of gasoline, my need for her combusts.

I disengage her lips long enough for her to drop to her feet, then I turn and pick her up by her pert ass and devour her sweet berry lips. Camil moans unabashedly into my mouth and wraps her legs around me again. This time bringing her pussy against my stomach as she grinds against my abs. I growl into her mouth and thrust upward, but again it's not enough. Like a man drunk on his woman, I stumble to the couch I almost made my bitch and sit with Camil astride me. Our lips never part as Camil continues to grind her pussy against my denim-clad cock. It aches like a motherfucker to be inside her, and when I lift her off me to undo my belt and pants, she doesn't hesitate to stand and remove her pajamas, not sparing me a moment to take her in before she's back in my lap, pussy bare, hand reaching for my cock. She lifts my tip to her weeping cunt, and with a Cheshire cat smile, she drops down hard, planting my dick deep in her heat.

"Fuck!" I bellow into the room, my head slung back, eyes rolling from the rapture of her pussy fisting my cock.

"Oh, God, Bo. It feels..." I palm her juicy hips, lift her ass, then slam into her from beneath. "Aaaah!"

"It feels. Fucking. Incredible," I punctuate each word with a hard thrust, each one causing Camil's magnificent breasts to bounce in front of my face. Her nipples are peaked and ripe for the picking. My mouth covers one berry while my fingers pinch and twist the other. She yelps when I give the nipple in my mouth a harsh bite, but it doesn't stop her from grinding against me as I jackhammer into her sweet pussy. The air is charged with our sex-crazed energy and perfumed with our desire while echoes of our shared moans and grunts play as the soundtrack to our coming together.

Camil's hips begin an uneven rhythm, and the walls of her pussy start to flutter around my cock. My flower is close. And thank God for it because I'm close to embarrassing myself with how soon I am to coming like a teenage boy his first time.

As it is, I grit my teeth and double my efforts to make my sweet flower glow with ecstasy. I fist the sweat-soaked locks of her hair until her lashes flutter open and her stormy gray eyes lock with mine.

"Keep your eyes on me, *fiore.*" I lift her until I'm barely breaching her pussy. "You ready?" I rasp, and with her lazy nod, I lock my teeth around her nipple, pinch her clit and slam her down on my swollen cock.

"Bo!" she screams my name as her body convulses on top of mine while my own body locks up as I ride the euphoric wave with her. My grip on her hips is bruising, but this sweet, sweet release has me immobile, my vision fuzzy at the edges, and her moans become faded echoes as my cock empties inside her.

When my body finally unlocks, I pull Camil's limp body to lay against my chest, where she buries her face in my neck as though she's done it a million times. We sit like that while the sweat cools on our skin, and I've drawn a cluster of abstract figures across her back. Camil shivers in my arms, and I curse myself when I realize it's from the icy cold breeze still blowing in from the shattered window, a reminder of my loss of control and the reason behind it. The reminder of my abandonment of her to the deviants of the Idris Calvano household––unknowingly or not. Then there was her betrayal. She ran. She left Dom drugged and so despondent that he barely spoke a word after I found him knocked out on the couch. She left us with nothing more than a mouthed apology spoken into a bank camera. She left me, and I don't give a shit about her excuses.

Slowly I pull from her warmth and rearrange her on my lap to lift her bridal style. Her teeth chatter as I carry her to the room and place her on the bed before I throw the heavy quilt over her shoulders. "Stay here. I'll get the tub going, and while you're soaking, I'll start a fire and have Dom help me board up the window," I say robotically without so much as a glance her way. I can't look at her right now. Not while so many conflicting emotions coat my insides like oil.

Yes, I plan on marrying her whether she likes it or not, and she didn't stop me from taking her just now. Still, I need to keep her at arm's length until I can trust she won't run; otherwise, I'm likely to lock her away, throw away the key, and not feel an ounce of remorse for it.

"Okay," she murmurs with a hint of disappointment coating her tone. I keep fucking things up with her, but I don't have time to coddle her. I need to get her warm and then get the fuck away from her for a while. I put my phone on speaker and call Dom while I fill the large clawfoot tub with steaming warm water.

"You're still alive?" He must pull the phone away from his mouth because his following words are distant. "Hey Lorenzo, I owe you a hundred bucks. He's still alive."

I hear Lorenzo curse in the background before Dom gets back on the line. "You fucking bet against me, asshole?"

I can hear the shrug in his voice. "I've seen what Camil can do. I had a fifty-fifty shot. So, if you don't need someone to speak at your funeral, what's up?"

I curse the man in our mother tongue and run a hand through my hair. "I need you to board up the kitchen window while I go into town to see if they can order a new pane of glass." I don't go into detail, and Dom doesn't ask. *Good man.*

"I think they have some scrap wood out in the shed on the property. Give me twenty minutes."

"Fine. Have Lorenzo come to watch Camil," I order, then disconnect.

"Calling over my babysitter?" I turn at Camil's angry voice from over my shoulder, still wrapped in the quilt, her hair knotted and tangled at the nape of her neck, her lips red and swollen from my kisses.

"Yes," I answer emotionlessly when I'm anything but. In fact, *too many* emotions are clouding my head right now that I wouldn't be surprised if my brain and heart didn't give out.

I shut off the water and extend my hand to help her into the tub. Her gray eyes narrow, and when she shrugs off the heavy quilt, I have to swallow the saliva pooling in my mouth at her naked body on full display.

Fuck, she is incredible with her olive skin, cut arms from her strength training, and perfectly round breasts. Hours of yoga have given her a tight waist with a four-pack of abs that flare from wide hips down to her neatly trimmed mound that leads to a tight little cunt.

"Come," I say around the lump in my throat.

She takes my offered hand and steps one foot and then the other into the tub. Steam billows around her as she settles beneath the water and sighs in contentment. "Aaahh, this feels so nice." My dick goes from stiff to a steel pipe that I don't bother to hide, and like the temptress she is, Camil licks her lips, her eyes locked on my cock bulging beneath my unbuttoned jeans. "You can go now." She brushes me off with a flick of her wrist, then sinks below the water's surface—little *minx.*

I don't wait for her to re-emerge from the water. Instead, I shake my head and enter the bedroom to start a fire. The room has gone from chilly to just below comfortable when hammering comes from the front of the house. I walk into the living room to dress back in my discarded shirt that smells like Camil and button my jeans. My eyes flick back to the couch where only moments ago I fucked my flower, and I have to adjust my still erect cock to get the zipper of my jeans up.

Exhaling a heavy breath, I put the images aside—— or at least attempt to——grab my heavy jacket and meet Dom outside the kitchen window where he's already finished nailing in the thick board.

"I'm not even going to ask," he says before picking up another board to use inside the cabin.

"Good man," I return and meet Lorenzo at the door. "She's relaxing now. She's free to move around the house, but she is *not* to step foot outside the cabin. Got it?"

"Got it, Boss." Lorenzo salutes, and with his confirmation, I head to town under the guise of ordering a pane of glass when in actuality, I'm running like a fucking coward.

Two birds, one stone.

14

Camil

I *had sex with Bo.*
For the love of God, I had sex with Bo! But not just sex, mind-bending, reality-squishing, proof of God's existence sex... and then he went ice cold on me. He couldn't even look me in the eye. Was it not good for him? No, that couldn't be it. I don't have a brothel of past lovers, but I had my wild days and learned some things after his harsh rejection on the beach all those years ago. Those men were just test subjects to hone my skills and learn to please a man, so I would blow Boian's mind when this exact day came. His bellow of release nearly busted an eardrum and sent my womanly pride skyrocketing, only to plummet to the ground in a fiery mess when he turned from scorching hot to iceberg chilly after coming down from his high. Maybe it isn't a lack of skill, but that it's *me*. I know he cares about me, but am I overestimating his feelings for me? Does he truly see me as more of a sister, and it freaked him out that we had sex?

"Ugh," I groan and stand from the now lukewarm water. The towel on the rack is threadbare and itchy, but I don't mind. It reminds me of the years I lived in the servant's quarters at Idris's home in Rome. The blankets he provided were nearly see-through, and the towels were barely big enough to cover my then-lanky body. Idris loathed our very existence, but who else was going to serve him? Yes, I was made to serve the household even though my father was a loyal soldier to Idris, but I didn't care. It kept me busy, and Layla, one of the older maids at the time, assigned me the jobs that kept me out of sight for the most part.

I never bothered to reveal any of it to anyone because there's no point in bringing up things that couldn't be changed now. Idris and the guard that liked to use me as a punching dummy were dead, and the others were given a choice: pledge allegiance to Emiliano or eat a bullet. I was just thankful I wasn't raped in all those years trapped in that house. It was a sad day when you were grateful for the beatings so long as they kept the sexual violations at bay.

Shaking the useless thoughts away, I finish drying myself and then go about the task of combing through my thick waves. The comb catches more than once, and I grit my teeth with each tug. I need a trim, but remembering the shaggy, unkempt hair of the men in town and the women with long braids, I have a feeling a haircut is a task done by oneself around here, and a search of the small pedestal sink drawers confirms what I suspected. Taking the pair of brand-new hair-trimming scissors and another towel to cover my shoulders, I split my hair down the middle and bring the heavy sections over each shoulder. Years of trimming my own hair make quick work of the dead frizzy ends, but when I should place the scissors down, I find myself cutting more... and more and more. Until my once waist-length hair barely skims the tops of my breasts. I smile at my new reflection as I pull away the rivers of dark strands. My head feels lighter, and my scalp itches slightly now that the heavy burden has been removed.

I finish up evening some sloppy ends, comb through what's left, then with a hum on my lips, I gather up the remnants of my hair and toss them in the small waste basket by the sink, then take my time getting dressed in long thick leggings with a hidden weapons compartment sewn in––like all my garments––and an oversized Dallas Stars sweater Greta gifted me after catching me watching American football.

I smile as I remember Greta gasping and clutching invisible pearls as though she caught me torturing puppies and lectured me about how hockey–– notably Dallas Stars hockey––was the only sport worth watching, then promptly demanded one of the guards to order me this sweater. It didn't matter that, at the time, she was still considered a prisoner. She looked her guard in the face, gave him her don't-mess-with-me stare and the big brute scurried off to do her bidding.

I laugh, and my heart thrills with the sudden realization that I can attend Emil and Greta's wedding now that I've been found. I should be pissed that my plan to escape the Roma mafia life failed––and

I am, if only for my pride––but a larger part of me knows I wouldn't have been able to stay away from my friend's wedding.

With a resolute sigh, I finish dressing, place my butterfly knife in the hidden pocket, don my favorite chunky hiking boots, and exit my room. Each step I take is met with the sting of Boian's thick intrusion between my thighs, and despite his earlier dismissal, my smile magnifies times ten.

"Uh oh, what did you do to warrant that grin?" Lorenzo studies me like a parent who got a call from the principal. "Did you set your room on fire, booby trap the place to explode at any wrong move, hide poison––"

"Shut up, Enzo." I slap my would-be babysitter's chest, and Lorenzo groans at my nickname for him. "Can't a girl be happy to be surrounded by three strapping men? Oh, we could have a night of strip poker." I waggle my eyebrows, and Lorenzo bursts into laughter.

"Yeah, let's see how well that goes down with the boss. Boian would torture us and then slit our throats if we even suggested a game that removes so much as one of your socks."

I give him a cheeky grin. "I wasn't planning on losing." Lorenzo is all too aware of my poker skills and has lost hundreds of his hard-earned money to me.

His face scrunches up like he smells something unpleasant. "Yes, well, I don't think he would be too happy with us getting naked in front of you either."

I shrug. "He's not my father or my husband, so he doesn't get a say in whom I see naked."

"Pfft, okay, Camil. Continue to think that, and you're in for a rude awakening." He shakes his head like I'm a complete imbecile, invoking my temper to heat at his condescension.

"What the fuck does that mean?" I take a threatening step toward the giant man.

Lorenzo holds his hands up in surrender. "Hey, calm down."

Wrong answer.

I spring forward to get in the brute's face——well, I get in his chest because the guy is as tall as a pine——and my eyes narrow. "Did you just tell me to calm down?"

His eyes volley between mine, and if I'm not mistaken, sweat breaks out along his brow. "I was just——" I silence his explanation with a lift of my hand.

"First of all, don't ever tell a woman to 'calm down.' Second, you and Boian can go to hell if you think he controls what or *who* I do." I don't give him a chance to retort. Grabbing my heavy puffer jacket, I swing open the door. At the same time, Dom steps onto the porch with an overly zealous flourish to his voice.

"Where are you off to?" he asks with a smile, but he can't hide the low grumble of warning in his tone.

"I'm going for a walk in the forest. I do it every day to get used to the elements," I answer dismissively and go to walk by him, but he steps in front of me, a solid brick wall meant to keep me at bay.

"Sorry, Camil. The boss says you have to stay inside." He has the decency to look apologetic, and I hate what I'm about to do, but...

"It's okay, Dom. I understand," I say in a saccharine sweet voice and clutch his shoulder in a reassuring gesture. It's the only warning he gets before my foot buries itself in his groin. Dom's eyes go wide as my foot makes contact with his dick, and when he clutches himself with one hand while the other nearly splinters the wood of the doorframe, I take advantage of the opening to run past him and into the chilly morning air. The wind whips across my much shorter, still-damp hair and feels like tiny icicles stabbing my cheeks and chin, but I don't stop. I'm not even heading to the forest where I planned to go in the first place. Instead, I just run straight ahead, laughing in victory.

I glance over my shoulder and watch as both men stand there watching me, Dom's face flushed and his shoulders hunched in the lingering discomfort of having his balls relocated to his throat.

I turn and start jogging back words as I taunt the two brutes, "Too slow, boys!" But the moment matching grins stretch their lips, I know I fucked up. "Oh, shit," I squeak, then pivot to the side to change the direction of my getaway, but a solid arm wraps around my middle and yanks me up and against his chest with a steel grip.

"Going somewhere, baby?" Boian rasps against my ear, sending a zing to my clit and electricity to my nipples. I nearly groan at my body's reaction to my violet-eyed devil but tamp it down before it reaches my lips because I refuse to give in to this man again ... at least not without a fight.

If it were any other man, I could break his hold, but Boian taught me everything I know. Therefore, he knows all my techniques, so I decide to go the temper tantrum route and fling my arms back, grip the roots of his hair, and yank with all my might. "Let me go, Boian Greco!" the heel of my boots connects with his shin, and I mentally fist pump when I hear him let out a grunt of pain.

"Dammit, Camil, stop fighting me!"

"Never! You don't get to keep me locked away..." I gasp for air when he tightens his hold.

He jerks his head back and forth to dislodge my python-like grip in his silky waves. "Watch me!" he literally growls against my ear as he stomps back to the cabin with me still struggling and pulling at his scalp. "Take a break, guys. I've got it from here," he tells Lorenzo and Dom, who stand there grinning like lunatics.

"Sure thing, Boss." They give him a small salute and then make their way back to their cabin.

"You traitorous bastards!" I scream so loudly at their retreating forms that I wouldn't be surprised if I cause an avalanche.

Boian slams the cabin door and carries me to my room, where he not so gently drops me on the bed. I immediately spring back up and charge at him, my fist cocked.

THWACK.

My fist makes contact with his chin, and while his head barely moves with the hit, the bones in my hand feel like they're crumbling inside my skin. "Fuck! What is your chin made of, granite?" I shake out my hand, all thoughts about fighting him smothered by the pulsing ache in my hand. I'm so distracted by checking my hand for broken bones that I forget I'm supposed to be in attack mode.

But Boian forgets nothing and, with inhuman speed, grabs my uninjured wrist and whips me around. At the same time, he sits on the edge of the bed and wrenches me forward, eliciting a yelp from me as I fall over his lap with my ass in the air.

SMACK.

His hand comes down with an echoing smack, and I'm so stunned that it takes me a second to register the sting, but when I do, it's game on. I buck like a bull and kick like a mule, but Boian is too strong and skilled in hand-to-hand combat that in no time, he has my legs pinned under his and my wrist behind my back while my injured hand lays limp against the floor, throbbing from the hit and all the blood rushing to my fingertips.

"You spank me again, motherfucker, and I will gut you in your sleep!" I seethe and gasp with fury. But Boian is immune to my wrath and ignores my threat with another searing slap to my ass.

"Don't disobey, and you won't need to be punished," he grumbles, then brings his hand down again. "That one was for leaving the cabin when I gave specific instructions for you to stay put." *SMACK.* "That one's for the punch to the face." He punctuates his words with blistering swat that has my core grasping at nothing and my clit pulsing between my legs. "And this one's for hurting yourself." This time his hand lands with the searing heat of a branding iron, and tears leak from my eyes while my pussy begs to be filled.

When he releases me and pulls me into his chest, my ass burns against his thighs, and my pride is beaten to hell. But it's the tickle in my core and the slickness of my sex that has me clenching my eyes shut and snuggling into his warm body.

"That wasn't so bad, was it?" he whispers against my hair while he pets my back in long, tender strokes, juxtaposed to his harsh punishment. I shiver against his chest, and he squeezes me closer when I sniffle and bury my head in his neck. "Answer me, *mia fiore.*"

My nails pick at the ridges of his black Henley. "It hurt," I answer with half-truths because while yes, it hurt, it also felt incredible. After the initial burn, the pain melted into something different, like liquid heat running across my skin and landing in my core, making my sex wet and pulse for more. I've never explored impact play with past lovers. Not because I'm a prude or abhorrent to the idea––quite the opposite, actually. I just never trusted any of them enough to hand over that kind of control. Granted, I didn't hand it over to Boian either––he took it—but if there is one thing I know for sure, it's that I can always trust Boian with my physical well-being.

"That's the point of punishment, my flower." He nuzzles my hair and inhales deeply before exhaling on a sigh. "I will never go past your limits, but you will be punished for disobeying, Camil. It's only fitting after you punished us by running." I lift my head to argue, but he silences me with a finger to my lips and a warning look. "No, don't bother arguing. What you did was cruel. Not to mention stupid, and won't be tolerated or go unpunished."

The vein in my neck pulses heavily with my desire to tell him where he can shove his punishment, but I think better of it when he tips up a dark eyebrow with a promise of another punishment——a punishment that I may not enjoy so much this time.

I swallow the colorful euphemism I have locked and loaded and focus on Boian's violet eyes. I trace the long white scar that mars his chiseled features with trembling fingers. I don't know if I'm trembling in rage or maddening lust. Either way, I don't like it. It makes me feel weak.

"What exactly does that mean?" I ask around the desert in my throat.

Boian tucks a strand of hair behind my ear. "You cut your hair," he points out.

I take his hand in mine. "Answer the question, Bo."

His lips tip up slightly. "I love it when you call me that." He brushes away the lock of hair from my face. "What it means is that if you wish to make it to Greta and Emil's wedding walk in two weeks, then you will do as I say when and how I say it."

I can feel the blush of my boiling anger creep across my cheeks at his archaic threat, pin my temperance from before falls away. "So, you say jump, and I say how high?" I chuckle darkly, but there is no humor in his dark violet eyes.

"That's exactly right," he answers without hesitation or remorse, and my vision goes red. I move to dislodge myself from his arms, but he's having none of it. "Steady yourself, Camil."

"Let go of me, Boian. I am not one of your brain-dead drooling women you can command to heel." I wiggle and jerk in his lap but freeze when he hisses and bites his bottom lip. It's then that I notice his erection pressing against my ass.

"Easy, baby. Keep grinding on my cock, and I'll have you on your knees and my cock down your throat."

My thighs squeeze together instinctually, looking to relieve the building pressure in my core, and I have to swallow the saliva pooling on my tongue. *Great, now I am one of those drooling women.*

"Mmm," he hums and trails the tip of his nose across my cheek to my ear, "*Mia fiore* likes the idea of me deep-throating her." He bites my earlobe before soothing the sting with a gentle kiss. "And you're right. You're not like those other women. You're stronger. Smarter. And a hell of a lot more precious to me." He punctuates each statement with a kiss on my shoulder, but it's his words that have my heart thudding heavily and my chest warming like the sands of Olbia in July.

Still, I want to argue that if I'm so precious to him, why did he leave me all those years ago? But I remind myself that the past needs to stay in the past. I clear the lump in my throat to ask, "So, we are returning for Emil and Greta's wedding?"

He lifts his head from my shoulder with the sweetest smirk and traces a finger along my bottom lip absent-mindedly as he speaks, "That all depends on you. Can you do as you're told and trust me? Or throw a fit whenever I say something you disagree with and miss your best friend's special day? I mean," he tilts his head to the side, "you didn't plan on showing up in the first place, right?" he finishes with poignant sarcasm that has my temper simmering again, but not at him––well, not *just* at him––but at myself for even considering not attending Emil and Greta's wedding. If I'm being honest, I'm mad at myself for running too. But Boian doesn't need to know that.

So instead of admitting fault, I cross my arms over my chest and tip my chin in defiance. "You can stop with the passive-aggressive remarks, Boian. It doesn't suit you."

He grips my chin between his thumb and fore-finger, all remnants of lust gone. In its place is the severe mafia capo I've come to know over the years. "This is your last warning, Camil. Keep up with the insolence, and not only will you not be able to sit for days, but you will miss our friends saying their vows." He brings us nose to nose as he grumbles, "Am I clear?"

All I can do is stare back into his unusual eyes and grumble back an indignant, "Yes."

Like Doctor Jekyll and Mr. Hyde, his face goes from the stern stare of a capo to a boyish smile stretching his lips. "Good." He lifts me from his lap and then gives my already stinging ass a slap with a saucy wink.

"Ow." I swat his hand away, which only humors him more, and nothing can stop that smile from melting my heart and my lips from tipping up to mimic his. "You," I pluck a section of his beard between my fingers, and he winces when I pull on the remarkably soft whiskers, "need to trim that hedgehog you call a beard."

Boian lets out a hearty laugh, and I can't help but join him when his laughter has him bending at the waist with its boisterousness. "A hedgehog, huh." He heaves me into his chest, his laughter immediately dies, and his eyes go electric with carnal craving. "You won't mind this hedgehog when it's between your legs and rubbing against the soft skin of your thighs and pussy." He punctuates the crude word with a flick of his tongue across my top lip. Molten heat spreads across my skin, and if I were to die right now, I would have no regrets about those being the last words I ever hear.

He suddenly releases me from his hold and steadies me before he grabs my hand and drags me to the bathroom. "What are you doing?" I ask breathlessly.

"*I* am doing nothing. *You,* on the other hand, are going to give me a trim." He releases my hand and then lifts me to sit on the small lip of the counter before grabbing his grooming bag and pulling out his beard shaver.

He hands it to me, and I flick it on with a mischievous grin. "You sure you trust me not to give you a handle Fu Manchu mustache or the dreaded porn-stache?"

Boian wraps his arms around my waist and pulls me nose to nose with him. "Do your worst, Camil Radu."

15

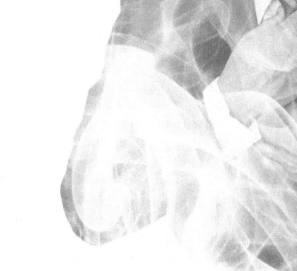

Boian

D amn, that woman.

Even indignant and fighting me every step of the way, she still has me by the balls with those stormy eyes, pillow-plump lips, and curves that make grown men cry for a taste. And if she hadn't had that trimmer in her hand and pressing against my skin, I would have been between her legs lapping up her sweet nectar.

The latter has a growl rumbling from my chest as I slice the vegetables for the *Ciorba de Perisoare,* Romanian meatball soup. With three men as big as Lorenzo, Dom, and me, I would have to buy Mr. Gheata's entire stock of vegetables, so I insisted the old shopkeeper give me the vegetables he planned to discard. Very few people know that the bits of discarded fruits and vegetables found in restaurant dumpsters are still edible if one knows what to look for. A helpful tip I learned while on a mission in Russia that lasted longer than expected, and food was scarce.

The mixture of beef meatballs, rice, various spices, and vegetables, all simmering in chicken broth, perfumes the air with a mouth-watering aroma. And it seems the smell wafting through the small cabin has the desired effect when Camil comes skidding into the small kitchen on socked feet, tight leggings, and that bright green sweater Greta gifted her. Her hair——though much shorter now——is stacked in large curls on top of her head, with rogue locks falling here and there. Her face is still masked with remnants of her previous petulance, but her stomach gives her no choice but to come out of her room as it grumbles loudly.

I chuckle when her cheeks pink in embarrassment and jerk my chin toward her phone sitting on the opposite. "Text Dom and Lorenzo to get their asses over for dinner."

"Oh, so I'm allowed to use my phone now?" She crosses her arms over her chest and cocks a hip.

I ignore her sarcasm this time and keep stirring the soup. "When I allow it, yes."

"Who the hell do you think I'll call, Bo? *Gesù Cristo!*" She stomps off to grab her phone, and I let out an irritated sigh but inwardly relish in her feistiness. Still, after having this argument for the tenth time since I took her phone from her this morning, I'm one second away from throwing the damn thing into the fire.

I set the soup to warm, then turn to her, my arms crossing over my chest, and I don't miss how her eyes run a path over my torso. I'm dressed in a long-sleeve Henley that fits snugly around my muscles that

95

stretch the fabric enough to show the hard definition of my biceps and shoulders. Camil has always had a thing for my arms, a fact I take advantage of when I flex my bicep just for the fun of watching her pupils dilate with desire.

"You tell me, Camil."

"Wh...What do you mean?" she asks with sincere curiosity, so mesmerized by my arms that she forgets her previous question.

"I mean, either you had the plan to run in your head long enough to plan everything down to the T, or you had help. If you had help, I can't trust you not to call that person to help you again. So, which is it?" I know Camil didn't need help to pull off her escape. The woman is smart, crafty, and resourceful all on her own, but I can't help baiting her. I'm itching to see the silver flame ignite in her eyes. That look of murder gets me hard every time, and the thought of punishing her makes the beast inside me howl.

But when I stare into those eyes, waiting for her to bite back, Camil surprises me by shrugging and starts typing the message to the guys. "He was nice enough to offer assistance, so who am I to turn it down?"

I huff out a humorless laugh. "You're such a little liar, *fiore*." And *she is* lying. Still, even the thought of another man aiding in her running––running from *me*––puts my teeth on edge. *Well played,* mia fiore. "Sit down before your mouth gets you into trouble."

"Fine," she mutters with a string of Romanian curse words following in her path as she makes her way to the living room, where all four of us will have our meal.

The door burst open seconds later, and Lorenzo and Dom step in, smiling broadly and harrying each other. Something about who got laid more in school, Dom jeering that even not being out yet, he still got more ass than Lorenzo's ugly mug.

"At least someone is having a good time," Camil grumbles and slumps against the back of the couch like a petulant child.

"Oh, come on, Cami, it's not so bad." Lorenzo ruffles her already disheveled hair and receives a punch to the gut for his trouble.

"Says the captor," she returns, and I smirk as the two bicker back and forth.

"Hey, I'm just the goon. He," Lorenzo points in my direction, "calls the shots." He finishes with his hands up in a sign of surrender.

"Yeah, he does seem to have control issues, doesn't he?" I can feel the heat of Camil's eyes burning into my profile, but I ignore her jab because she's right—though I don't see it as an issue. In the military and the mafia, you must maintain control of every move you make and every word you speak, or people die—*at least people who aren't meant to die.*

I shake away the memory of that day in Mexico that threatens to consume me and ladle up heaping bowls of soup and freshly baked bread. I bring over two bowls with the loaf of bread perched on the rims and sit beside Camil before handing her one.

"What? We don't get the royal service?" Dom gripes, and I respond by flipping him the middle finger. They grab their food and sit at the small table in the corner of the kitchen, leaving Camil and me alone to eat.

I shovel a meatball in my mouth just as Camil's whispered prayer floats across the small space between us. Her head is bowed, her eyes closed as she says a blessing over her food.

When her eyes open and she raises her head, her eyes latch onto mine. "What?"

I shrug. "Nothing. I didn't know you still prayed over your food."

I take another bite, and she follows with a hearty bite before swallowing and saying, "Of course I do. I pray before bed too. Call me naïve, but I like the knowledge that there's someone up there who has my best interest at heart." I hum absently around my spoon. "I pray for you too, you know. Especially the years you were away. I would find myself praying for you at random times. Cleaning the bathrooms, cooking, when Idris..." She trails off and shoves another meatball in her mouth.

The soup turns to dirt in my mouth at the reminder of what that bastard did, and like the insensitive bastard I am, I answer her selfless confession with, "Save your prayers for someone worthy of them, *fiore*." and finish the last spoonful of my soup. Standing, I take my bowl and offer to take hers, but she shakes her head and follows me to the kitchen, where we work together in silence to clean up. Lorenzo and Dom are back in their cabin after devouring their food like it was their last meal because, in this world, it very well could be.

"You are worthy even if you don't believe it," Camil says almost too quietly for me to hear ... but I do. My chest warms, and little jolts of pleasure prick at the stone encasing my heart.

After everything she's seen, every bloody mob war, assassination, torture, and my own dismissive treatment of her these past years, she still sees the good within the monster. It's one of the things I lo—I refuse to finish the thought. It's too dangerous. Whether it's more dangerous for her or me? I can't answer that.

Nonetheless, I refuse to put that burden on *mia fiore*, so sticking with my asshole behavior, I drop the rag on the counter and turn from her. "Go to bed, Camil." Then I walk away because the bars surrounding the beast begin to quiver, and I don't know what will happen if he escapes while I'm around her.

Not bothering with my coat, I walk out into the frigid air and inhale an icy breath, then exhale a plume of warm vapor. The beast calms but is never subdued with every deep inhale and exhale. He's always there, gripping the bars of his cage, desperate to break free and consume everyone in his path.

My ass hits the small wooden landing, my boots sink into the thick snow below, and for the first time, I debate whether or not forcing Camil to marry me is the right thing to do.

Initially, I never doubted that putting my ring on her finger was the best way to keep her safe, that marrying her was in her best interest when really it was about me and the feeling of terror, of being paralyzed with fear when I got the call from my surveillance team that she was missing. It was the closest I ever came to losing my mind and throwing open the cage to let the beast out to kill every one of my men that let her slip through their fingers. And God forbid my deepest fear came true, and she was taken away from me permanently. Only after I burned this Godforsaken world to the ground would I take my own life and accept the punishment of an eternity in hell.

My morbid thoughts are interrupted by the crunching of boots in the snow, and like the skilled soldier I am trained to be, I pull the tactical knife I always keep on me and swiftly pivot toward the sound.

"Whoa there, Boss. It's just me." Dom steps out of the shadow and into the moonlight carrying a stack of wood. "We were running low, so I thought I would stop by and see if you needed any."

I nod and sheath my knife before sitting back down, resolute to suffer in silence.

16

Camil

Asshole!

Once again, he shuts down and goes ice cold on me. Sure, I was poking at a nerve that had the potential to make him the least bit vulnerable with me, but with his reaction, you would think I am asking him to open his chest and pour out his life's blood.

Stubborn man.

Boian Greco was never the sappy type––far from it––but when it came to me, he readily let himself smile, laugh, and show at least a smidge of affection––until he returned from his extended military service. The moment he walked through the door, I knew he had changed. His face held a permanent scowl, his shoulders were tense, and he had a come-near-me-and-I'll-slit-your-throat vibe oozing from his pores.

The Bo I knew is dead, and in his place is the brutal, apathetic, insanely sexy, lost man. That was the other thing I noticed about him when he came home––though he tried hard to disguise it. But I could see past the iron wall in those violet eyes to the man lost in a nightmare because I saw it in my own eyes every morning after a beating.

My eyes sting at the thought of what he went through during his time away. Did they hurt him, torture him? Did he lose close friends ... or a lover? Is that why he shuts down every time we start to get close? The thought of him touching, kissing, *loving* another woman enough to keep himself at a distance from me makes me sick to my stomach, but also sad for him.

Kicking off the heavy quilt with an irritated *humph,* I pull myself to the edge of the bed and am about to lower myself to the floor for some midnight yoga when I hear loud whimpering sounds from outside the cracked bedroom door.

Pets were never allowed in the Calvano homes growing up—a fact I was on board with, if only for the animal's safety because Idris and his men would have had no reservations about using a beloved pet as collateral or worse. Emil was the same way at the beginning. He hated Rooster and only allowed him in his home to use against Greta, so I kept Rooster with me when he wasn't allowed to be with her. It wasn't until Emil heard what Rooster did when his human was being assaulted that Emil saw Rooster as more than a bargaining chip. Now the two are inseparable––much to Greta's chagrin.

Worried that an animal made its way inside the cabin through the boarded window, I forego my late-night yoga in search of the wounded creature. I tiptoe from my room and down the hall, where more whimpers followed by angry grunts pepper the air, and this time I recognize the sounds that I had become all too familiar with during my time in Idris's home, and they're not from an animal. I come to an abrupt halt at the living room threshold and watch as Boian's head thrashes side to side like he's searching for something … or someone. His brow is furrowed and lined with perspiration, his fist clenching at his sides as his thrashing becomes almost violent.

"No more. Leave her alone!" he whimpers loudly, his torso contorting like he's being held down.

My heart splinters and tears sting my eyes, and before I can talk myself out of it, I rush to Boian's side. "Bo, wake up," I order softly, but he doesn't respond, and his breaths become labored the longer he's stuck in the nightmare. I place a trembling hand on his clammy cheek and lean into his ear to whisper, "It's me, Bo, your flower. Please hear my voice and wake up. Come back to me, Bo. I need you." As though those three words are his trigger, Boian's eyes fly open, and his hand goes around my throat in a deadly hold. I yelp and fall back, with him following to sit astride me. The coffee table tips over, and my hands grapple with his around my throat, but soon instinct kicks in, and I give up attempting to dislodge his steel-like hold, instead opting to conserve my energy and, by proxy, my breath.

"I told you I'd kill you if you touched her!" he bellows to the imaginary enemy he's seeing.

"Bo…" I choke under his hold. Tears stream down his face as he works to kill the person he thinks I am.

I'm seconds from blacking out when I feel the knife Boian used to cut our bread at dinner, and though the thought of hurting him guts me, my will to live beats out any guilt I may suffer later.

I clutch the hilt of the knife, and just like he showed me before he left for the military, I thrust the small knife between his ribs, and thank God it has the desired effect. Boian grunts, and his hold on my throat loosens as I pull the knife from his side and push him with all my might. He topples to the side with a curse, then lifts to his hands and knees, one hand pressing against his wound.

It isn't until he hears me hacking and gasping for air beside him that his eyes swing to mine, and he blinks away the nightmare to finally see *me*. "Camil? What the fu..." His words screech to a halt, and his eyes widen as he takes in my disheveled state. He rushes to me on all fours and takes my face in his hands. "Fuck, Camil. I... Why did..."

He can't seem to speak in clear sentences, so I speak instead. "It's okay, Bo. You were having a nightmare. I know better than to wake someone when they're having one––"

"No shit," he scolds and has the decency to look chastised when I glare in reprimand.

"But you were contorting and calling out. I couldn't leave you like that," I croak one last time and fall to my ass.

Boian's hands drop from my face only to dive into his sweaty black waves. "Damn it, Camil, I could have hurt you." I wince and drop my gaze, but Boian has none of it. With a pinch of my chin, he lifts my head to return my eyes to his. "I didn't hurt you, right?" he asks hesitantly, but I never get to answer when his eyes drop to my throat, and suddenly he's crab-walking away from me like I'm diseased. "I did that? I fucking did that?" It's a rhetorical question because the look of horror in his eyes tells me he already knows the answer. He brings his elbows to his raised knees, and his hands dive back into his hair.

Ignoring the burn in my throat and the ache in my back, I slowly crawl over to him like he's the wounded animal I thought him to be earlier. I pull on his forearm, but he flicks me away, and though I know he's just mad at himself, my chest aches at his rejection. "Bo?"

"Don't, Camil." He lifts bloodshot wrathful eyes to me. "Listen to your voice. Go look at your fucking throat, then see if you want to touch me!"

I shrug and ignore the pain the slight movement causes in my shoulders. "You were having a nightmare, and I knew the risks."

That has him chuckling humorlessly and running a hand over his cropped beard. "Stop making excuses for me nearly ... killing you." The latter is choked, and my heart completely crumbles.

Again, ignoring my aching body, I lean forward and wiggle between his bent knees, and this time he doesn't dare rebuke me. "What are you doing, Camil?"

His hands fall to his sides, and I take the opportunity to straddle his lap and bring my arms around his head. "Don't push me away, Bo. Please, not right now." I bring my lips to his neck and feel him shiver

105

beneath me. His arms go around me, and he crushes me to him in a hold full of desperation.

His cheek presses against my breast while I hum lightly. "The most beautiful sound."

"My humming?" I snicker, very aware that I'm a horrible singer.

"Hearing your heartbeat. Life." He holds me tighter, and I don't even care that I can barely breathe.

We sit like that for I don't know how long. My knees ache, and my legs are officially numb, but I refuse to interrupt this moment by complaining. "I'm sorry I stabbed you," I mumble against his neck.

He stiffens beneath me, and I lift my head to watch the multitude of emotions play in those violet orbs. "Don't apologize. I'm proud of you for doing what you needed to do to save your life." He tucks a lock of hair behind my ear before running coarse fingertips over my cheek, down my jaw, then over my throat, where bruises no doubt have begun to bloom. "I'm so fucking sorry it's me who instigated it. I will never forgive myself, Camil."

As he speaks, I notice that the longer we sit here, the paler he becomes. I brush a lock of hair from his forehead. "Then I will forgive you for the both of us even though there's nothing to forgive. Now," I uncurl his arms from around me and stand, trying and failing to hide a wince because Boian misses nothing, "let's get that wound stitched up." I extend my hand to help him up.

He hesitates before shaking his head and pulling himself up. This time I don't take offense. His brow crinkles, and he twists to the side to take in his bloody shirt. "Damn, *fiore,* you got me good." He smiles down at the bloody mess like a proud papa before lifting his eyes back to mine.

With a haughty air in my tone, I lift my chin in superiority. "Of course I did, and I'm insulted by your surprise," I finish, then sashay off toward my bedroom, a smile tipping my lips and Boian's laughter trailing behind me.

17

Boian

I fucking hate that Camil saw me in the throes of a
nightmare. Weak and vulnerable. But with every
pulse of pain that runs up my side from where she
stabbed me, I can't help but feel anything but pride. I
may have taught her how to protect herself, but she's
the one that has to lift and use the knife. And use it
she did––with a surgeon's accuracy, no less.

After stitching up my wound, I head to the bathroom to clean off the cold sweat still clinging to my
skin, but stop short when I find Camil standing at the
sink ... naked as the day she was born and soaking her
bloody nightshirt in the basin.

She looks at me from over her shoulder with a
coy smile. "Did you need something, Bo?"

I shift on my feet. "I..." Jesus, she is glorious. Soft
in all the right places and hard and toned in the others.
Speaking of hard, my dick could drive nails right now,
watching her ass shake as she scrubs at her nightshirt,
the slightest peek of the side of her breast...

"Bo!"

I blink and mumble, "Huh?" like an *idioto* and look back to her eyes that glow knowingly. Mentally shaking myself, I jerk my chin toward the tub. "I need to rinse off." She nods but doesn't move from her spot at the small counter and returns to scrubbing at the blood stain on her shirt.

I undress while the tub fills and discard my bloody T-shirt. Even if I could get the blood out, there's still the matter of the small slit from the knife. I toss it in the bin, check the water temperature, then sink into the almost scalding hot water. The tub isn't nearly big enough for my six-three height, and I have to bring my knees up to where the water hits the tops of my calves, and my back is plastered against the porcelain edge just to fit. *What I wouldn't give for a shower.*

Steam rises from the water's surface, and I breathe it into my lungs, allowing it to ease the tension in my muscles. My wound burns like a son-of-a-bitch, but the pain is nothing compared to the pride I feel for my flower for doing what it took to save herself.

"Here, lay your head back." Camil's hand brushes over my sweaty hair, and I do as she says without hesitation. She takes the cup from the sink, fills it with warm water, and slowly pours it over my hair. Once my hair is saturated, she takes my three-in-one shower gel and begins massaging it into my scalp, and I don't bother to suppress my groan of pleasure. Camil giggles above me, then kisses my forehead, and something inside me splinters. Is it the stone around my heart? Or my sanity? Either way, it sends warmth through my chest and pulses of dopamine through my veins.

My cock lengthens and breaches the water's surface. She rinses my hair before taking a cloth and washing my chest, going lower with each sweep of her hand. "Camil," I growl and reach an arm out to palm the back of her head and bring our lips a breath away from each other. "Come sit on my cock, baby." I lick her bottom lip, then bite on the plump berry. Camil gasps at the sting of my bite, then moans into my lips.

Too soon, she pulls away, and when my cock stiffens further at the vision of her riding it hard and fast, Camil does neither. Instead, she puts on a baggy T-shirt and ugly plaid pajama pants before she grabs a towel and stands above me expectantly. "There will be none of that until your stitches come out."

I laugh at her ridiculousness, then frown at her narrowed gaze. "You're serious? Camil, *fiore*, I've fought in wars with much worse."

"Those were situations that couldn't be helped. We're not at war. Though I can definitely make it feel like we are." She smiles and tips her head in a try-me-motherfucker look. When I stand and get out of the tub, her smile turns victorious but drops altogether when I bend and haul her over my shoulder. "What the hell, Boian? What do you think... Ow!" she yips when my hand lands with a crack on her plaid ass.

I stomp across the room, my side burning like a motherfucker. "You don't make the rules, baby." I drop her unceremoniously to the creaky bed, and she immediately scrambles to her knees to turn and scold me, but I have both her ankles shackled in my hands and her face planted into the mattress, and she screams out her frustration. I take the opportunity to straddle her hips, my ass sitting on the small of her back with a glorious view of her plaid-covered ass.

I slide down the plaid pants and expose her creamy flesh. "Don't you fucking dare, Boian Greco," she threatens, and I love how her accent gets thicker when she's pissed. "I swear I will slit your throat next time I have a knife in my hand!"

She bucks beneath me, and I just smile at her fight and swivel my hips to rub my cock between her ass cheeks. "I have no doubt you will try, *mia fiore*, but I warned you to obey me, or there would be consequences." With that, I bring my hand down on her pert ass. Her hips jut upward with the hit, prompting my cock to rub along her skin. I groan and fist my cock to keep the bastard from exploding right here and now.

"You son-of-a-bitch!" she yells into the mattress, but I only laugh harder when she presses her thighs together to relieve the pressure in her pussy that's no doubt wet and aching.

"That gets you four more."

"What? You--" I silence her protest with two more slaps in quick succession. Her ass cheeks clench, and the imprint of my hand blooms a rosy red on her smooth olive skin.

I bring down the last two strikes, and by the time the last one hits, I'm hard as stone and gulping for air. I free her from my hold and flip us both so I can dive on top of her for a punishing kiss. She delivers in kind as she tears at my lips with her teeth. I rip the shirt over her head and watch her skin pebble with goosebumps. I don't take the time to warm her up——not that I need to when her pussy is coating my cock with her nectar. With one thrust, I bury myself to the hilt. Camil winces at my intrusion but moans in ecstasy because my *fiore* is a dirty little minx who likes a bite of pain with her pleasure. The fact has me unhinged and thrusting inside her like a madman. My head swims as I gulp and gasp, matching Camil's strangled breaths below me. She claws at my arms, bleeding me, claiming me. It's her claiming that sets me off. My balls draw up, and with one final thrust, I bellow her name as my cock pumps her tight canal full of my seed, coming so hard it borders on painful.

Camil purrs and lifts her hips beneath me, coaxing me to keep going. With a satisfied smile and a heavy sigh, I kiss the tip of her nose, then bring my lips to her ear to whisper, "It wouldn't be a punishment if you got want you wanted in the end, would it?"

I see the moment my words register, and I jump from the bed just as she swings at me. My dick is still hard, and I'm smiling like a loon as she stands on the bed in all her naked glory, flushed and sweaty.

"You bastard!" She leaps from the bed, and I don't waste time getting to the door and slamming it shut before she can land a hit.

The woman is a wildcat. And I fucking love it.

I stand outside the door waiting for her to come barreling from the room, but when I'm met with nothing but the stillness around me, I risk leaning my ear against the door, and what I hear makes my dick take notice and reach for the source of the low moans coming from the other side of the door. When Camil's sweet whimper of need penetrates the wood between us, I grasp my cock and bring the image of *mia fiore* lying on the bed, fingering her tight little cunt, to the forefront of my mind. My hand fists my cock tighter, and I have to bite my palm to keep the groan from breaching my lips. My eyes clench shut as I imagine her back arching from the attention she gives to her swollen clit while her other hand squeezes the soft globes of her breasts in tandem, twisting and pinching the tight peaks of her nipples.

"Oh God, Boian, yes! Boian, Boian, give it to me," she chants in her sexy, breathy voice, and I know my flower is close by the quickening of her pants and the long groan she releases.

I jerk my cock with punishing strokes and fall against the door with each pump of my fist. Camil's silver eyes stare back at me from behind my eyelids, her mouth agape with her moans. Tears coat her dark lashes with the euphoria engulfing her beautiful body as she sucks on her fingers and then shoves them inside her pussy to mimic the hard thrust of my cock.

"It's not enough, Bo. I need you. I need you to fuck me," she whines and grinds her sweet pussy against her hand.

"Keep going, *fiore*. Show me how you want me to fuck you," I grunt and tilt my head to the ceiling. Wave after wave washes over me, but I won't let it take me under until my flower comes. My back heats the wood of the door as I thrust into my fist and listen to Camil bringing herself to...

The door at my back opens, and I go from vertical to horizontal before I can catch myself. The breath gushes from my lungs as my back hits the bedroom floor.

I lay there with my dick still in my hand, staring at nothing, when a Camil-shaped shadow blankets my sex-fogged vision. When I blink her into focus, she stares at me with a look of pure innocence, but it's all an act. The cock-tease knows exactly what she just did. Her intentions are more apparent when she steps over my prone body, still sweaty and heaving from my unfulfilled jerkoff session, then turns with a saucy smirk. "Sucks to be left high and dry, doesn't it?"

18

Camil

He left me! He left me just out of reach of an orgasm. Yes, I finished myself off, but it was lackluster compared to the real thing. And the bastard knew exactly what he was doing.

But even after getting him back by denying him his own release, I toss and turn the rest of the night, managing only to get a few hours of sleep. So when I wake the next morning, my body is strung tight like a bow, and my brain is foggy––nothing a little fresh air won't cure. I get dressed in my warmest clothes and head into the living room, where Boian sits reading the newspaper with his feet propped up on the now-righted coffee table.

"I'm going into town," I throw over my shoulder and grab my jacket before opening the door and stepping out onto the small landing, but I don't make it a foot before being hauled back into the cabin and pinned against the door by Boian's massive body, and I curse my body when it immediately responds to his dominance.

"You're not going anywhere, Camil," Boian grumbles.

I roll my eyes and try to ignore the pulsing need to say, "Yes sir," and let him drag me to the couch, where he punishes me with a firm hand to my ass. "For the love of God, Bo, I'm not running! I'm just going into town to walk around and get some fresh air. I feel suffocated being stuck in this cabin twenty-four-seven." When he says nothing, I cup his bearded cheek and plead, "Please, Bo. You can trust me because I'm done running. I know where I belong."

His eyes search mine before finally he takes a step back and runs a hand through his dark locks. "Fine, but I'm going with you, and you are *not* to leave my side, Camil. Do you understand?" I want to balk at his highhandedness, but then my punishment from last night plays in my mind, and I swallow my pride and nod in agreement.

Boian grabs his jacket, and we leave the cabin, me following the path to town and Boian the shoveled path to the SUV. "We're walking, Bo," I call over my shoulder and chuckle when he growls and stomps toward me in a belligerent huff. "Don't be a baby. It's not that cold." I'm lying even as the tip of my nose blushes in the frigid air.

"It's not the cold I'm worried about," he mumbles from beside me.

I watch my feet as I trudge over the deeper sections of the freshly fallen snow. "What do you mean?"

Boian clutches my arm when my foot sinks deeper than I expect, and I nearly faceplant into the snow.

"Besides you being extremely clumsy?" he deadpans.

"Hardy har har. Yes, besides that."

He lets out a heavy sigh of frustration and runs his hand through his hair. "We have enemies, Camil. We aren't immune to the dangers of our world just because we relocate."

"I'm very aware, Bo." I kick a stick from the path. "Exactly how long were you trailing me? And why didn't you just approach me that day in town?" I ask, my eyes on the path beneath my feet, but when the sound of Boian's heavy steps cease, I turn to find him staring at me with twin violet flames of rage and ... fear. The latter has me scurrying to his side and swinging my head to look for whatever has him on guard. "What? What is it?" I look back at him when I don't see any apparent threat.

"I wasn't tracking you that day, Camil. The day I confronted you, I had just stepped off the plane and came straight to the cabin."

His words hit me like a heavyweight boxer's glove to the head. "You weren't following me?" I repeat around the fear clawing at my throat.

"No," he answers through clenched teeth before grabbing me by the arm, turning us, and stomping back to the cabin.

I stumble a few times, but Boian is quick to right me. "Would you slow down?" I gasp.

Fed up with my clumsiness, Boian turns and sweeps me into his muscular arms and presses me tightly against his granite-like chest. My arms instinctually circle his, and for once, I'm thankful for my clumsiness because with the fear currently wracking my bones, I don't think I could walk on my own much longer.

But my gratitude dissolves with every crunch of snow beneath his feet and every snap of a twig from the forest in the distance. "Do you really think our enemies are here? That they... they were watching me?" I whisper, but Boian doesn't speak, too focused on getting us to safety——getting *me* to safety. We're in the cabin with the door bolted shut in seconds. Still, a shiver runs along my spine that isn't from the chill outside. "Bo?"

I think he will continue to ignore me as he goes around the cabin checking windows and doors before finally turning to me with fierce violet eyes. "I wouldn't have brought Dom and Lorenzo if I felt we were the least bit safe, Camil, and now that I know you've been followed, I'm sure of it."

My teeth chatter with barely controlled panic while I try to convince myself that maybe I am exaggerating. Perhaps being completely alone was playing tricks with my mind. "Maybe I'm mistaken. Maybe it was someone smoking in the alley, and I took it for something else."

Boian stares at me with such a stupefied look that I would laugh if not for the knot of terror in my chest. "Bullshit, Camil. You don't make those types of mistakes, and your instincts rival my own." I squirm under his praise and the pride that paints his tone. "Now, tell me honestly. Do you believe you were mistaken?"

I don't bother to question myself again. Instead, I sigh in resolution. "No."

"Then don't second guess yourself. Especially when your life is on the line," he demands, his tone hard but not reprimanding.

"So, what now? Do we head back to Olbia?"

"No. I can't bring this to Emil and Greta's doorstep. I'll inform them of the situation, and we'll go somewhere off the grid." He pulls out his phone and starts typing out a message.

I look around the small cabin. "More off the grid than this? Are we going back to Switzerland?"

"No" is all he says, like I'll use the information to run again––at least, that's how it feels.

Well, screw that. I'm not letting him get away with giving me monosyllabic answers. "I'm going to need more than that, Bo. If we're not going home, then where are we going?" I ask, but he doesn't get to answer when I'm struck with a realization. "Wait. Does this mean we'll miss Emil and Greta's wedding?" It's the last thing I should be worried about, but it's one of the reasons I'm secretly happy Boian found me and the thought of not seeing my friends say their vows guts me.

"That's not my concern right now, Camil," Boian voices my unspoken words, and my heart sinks.

That's a yes.

"I know. You're right." I chew on my bottom lip and bring my hair over my shoulder to twist the strands around my finger.

Boian clasps the hand, twisting the strands of my hair into a knotted mess in his large warm hand, and

119

thumbs my lip from my teeth. "It's a wonder how you ever win at poker." He smiles despite the turmoil still dancing in his Alexandrite-hued eyes.

"What do you mean?"

"You bite your lip when you're contemplating, and you twirl your hair when you're afraid or nervous." My lips pucker in annoyance, and I shove at his rock-hard chest. He captures my hand and gently wrenches it behind my back. My back arches and my breasts press against his chest. We're so close I can feel his breath on my cheek when he speaks against my lips. "And," he continues, "you hold your breath right before you come."

A full-body shiver leaves me breathless, and the tender kiss Boian presses to my forehead has the fear and anxiety melting away. Something intentional on his part, I'm sure. I inhale a cleansing breath and exhale slowly a few times as the tension in my shoulders loosens, and my mind clears of everything but Boian and me in this moment together.

"I..." I clamp my mouth shut before I can finish my declaration and ultimately ruin the moment because, as I've come to learn, Boian isn't ready to hear those words from me.

19

Boian

I reluctantly pull myself out of our little bubble and release Camil from the circle of my arms. Her lips straighten into a thin line, and she crosses her arms over her chest protectively. My flower is disappointed, and though I'm not the sentimental type, I can still understand the importance of the man I consider a brother marrying the love of his life. But nothing is more important than Camil's safety, and I'm not risking Camil's life or willing to bring this danger to Emil's territory. Especially when I don't know where the threat is coming from. And that's the crux of the problem. The Calvano *famiglia* has enemies, but none have the connections, money, or an army large enough to take us on. So, the question is, who has the balls to come at us through our women? But it's a question that will have to wait until I debrief Emil and get Camil to a safe location.

I text Lorenzo to have the plane readied and for him and Dom to be prepared to head to the airport by sundown, to which he sends back a 10-4 without question. I'll brief them at the same time as Emil once Camil is secured on the plane and in the air.

"Go pack your things," I order Camil and pull my eyes from my phone when she doesn't move. Her brow is crinkled in contemplation, and her eyes narrow on something or nothing over my shoulder.

I'm waiting for the impending fit about my high-handedness when she surprises me when instead she asks, "Who do you think it could be?" Her voice is lilted with curiosity, and she wears the slightest pucker of her lips that tempts me to draw her into my arms and suck on the sweet berries.

Commanding my dick to heel, I puff out my cheeks and slowly release my breath. "I'm not sure. We've made more enemies of late by torching the warehouses and compounds of active sex slave trade groups. It could be that some of the vermin escaped the extermination. Though it's unlikely."

Camil's typical steel composure threatens to crack as she worries her bottom lip between her teeth. "Why is it unlikely?"

"Because wars are expensive, and none have the manpower or money to start and sustain a battle against the Calvano Roma."

She stares off into nothing and chews on her lip until a dot of crimson blooms on her petal-soft lip. She's anxious and literally tearing herself apart. "What if they have help? What if they ban together? Pool their resources..."

I take her face in my hands, wait until her eyes focus on mine, and then make her a vow. "I am going to find out who this is, Camil, and when I do, I will slice them open from throat to groin for daring to get close to you."

She cringes before her eyes go from a dark stormy day to a soft dove gray, and she brings a hand to the scar that runs down my forehead to disappear into my beard. With anyone else, the touch would send invisible bugs crawling across my skin. With Camil, it's like a shot of adrenaline to my dick.

"Will you tell me about this one day?" she asks, referring to the long scar that nearly cost me my sight, and a chill runs down my spine at the memory of how I got that scar. When I don't answer, she gives me a sad smile but doesn't press me to answer. Instead, she attempts to lighten the mood. "You're getting some gray hairs in your beard, old man." She tugs at the hair on my chin with a sassy grin.

I capture her hand and kiss the tips of each finger before biting down on her forefinger, then soothe the sting with a gentle lave of my tongue. "Careful, little girl. This old man bites."

Her pupils dilate, and she whimpers when I nip the palm of her hand. She watches me kiss, lick, and bite her palm like it's her sweet pussy laid out in front of me. "Promise?" she asks breathlessly.

I trail my lips to the bend of her elbow and suck the smooth skin into my mouth. "Mmm, I wouldn't lie to you, *mia fiore*," I say against her skin, and when I think she will let another sexy moan, her pants of desire freeze in her chest, and her skin goes red hot under my ministrations.

Her gray eyes light up with bolts of lightning before she jerks her arm from my grasp, not fazed by my warning growl. "You say you wouldn't lie to me, yet you lie to yourself and me every day."

My eyes narrow on hers, and I go to ask her what the hell she's going on about when Dom and Lorenzo choose that moment to come barreling in like bulls in a China shop. "The plane is fueled up and ready when you are," Dom announces to the room, his eyes swinging between Camil and me.

Keeping my glare pinned to my flower, I address Lorenzo and Dom. "Load up the SUV. Camil and I will be out in a minute."

"Already done, Boss. All except for yours and Camil's bags," Lorenzo returns, and for the first time since I became second in command, I wish my men weren't so efficient and well prepared.

When neither Camil nor I say anything further, both men read the room and leave Camil and me to stare at one another until her shoulders slump in defeat. "I'll go pack," she murmurs and slinks to her room. I hate seeing her this way, but we don't have time to get into personal shit right now, so I let her go to pack my things.

I text Emil that we have a situation and that I will contact him about it once we're airborne. He responds, "Don't get your ass killed, fucker." Emil's way of showing concern.

Camil packs quickly and is at the door as I'm holstering my gun. She eyes the weapon. "That reminds me. I want a gun," she says in a clipped tone.

I don't bother arguing. I nod and take her Rohrbaugh R9 pistol from my bag. "I figured you couldn't slip it onto a passenger flight, so I brought your favorite." I hand her the smaller pistol she preferred to shoot when I took her to the range back home, and she smiles down at the sleek weapon, her mood lifting.

"You remember," she says more to herself, but I respond nonetheless.

"Of course I do. I remember everything about you, Camil."

Her eyes shoot to mine, and her smile morphs into a sardonic tip of her lips. "Interesting." She doesn't elaborate as she opens the door, says a quiet goodbye to the little cabin, and stomps through the snow to the warmth of the waiting SUV.

The moment Camil is settled in her seat by the window, I debrief Dom and Lorenzo on the situation, and both get to work, whether contacting our men on the street to get the pulse on the underground or hacking into camera feeds, federal databases, or anything else Lorenzo deems necessary to crack open.

Once we've reached cruising altitude, I grab my bag from the overhead bin and open my laptop to dial Emil. It rings twice before he answers, his typical look of stoicism planted firmly on his face. Greta is sitting beside him, looking like the Roma queen that she has quickly come to embrace. "I assume every-thing went smoothly on your way to the airport?"

"Nothing out of the ordinary," I confirm.

"Good. Now, what the fuck is going on?" Emil gets straight to the point.

"The day we arrived, Camil had a shadow, and my gut tells me that shadow would have made their move this evening if we hadn't shown up."

"Has she seen them since?"

I shake my head. "She's been remanded inside the cabin most of the time."

"Pfft. Nice way of saying held captive," Camil mumbles to herself from her seat beside me while Emil and Greta don't even bother to suppress their matching grins.

Ignoring the trio, I continue, "After I confronted her at the cabin, she assumed I was the one shad-owing her, so she didn't mention the incident until this morning."

"Then it's safe to say she didn't get a good look at the person." This time it's Greta who speaks.

"Unfortunately, no," I confirm.

"Are you headed back to Olbia?" Greta's voice holds so much hope that it pains me to disappoint the woman who has become like a sister to me.

"I'm sorry, *mia regina,* but I don't feel that's best. I have a place near Dallas––"

"Dallas, Texas?" Greta smiles widely.

"It's the only Dallas I know of, *Signorina.*" I smile back, but it falls when I watch as understanding of what going to Texas means crawls across her face.

Her smile drops, and she chews on her thumbnail before asking the question to which she already knows the answer. "So, you guys won't be here for the wedding?"

"I'm sorry, but no." Camil sniffles beside me, and I catch her brush away a tear before I clutch her hand, tapping on the arms, and squeeze it in apology. She nods in acknowledgment but keeps her eyes directed out the window.

"I understand." Greta's melancholy voice pulls my eyes back to the video call. "Just do anything you have to do to bring her home safe and sound," our queen demands.

"Yes, *Signorina.*"

"I want updates at the end of each day. If you miss even one day, I will hunt you down and string you up like a slab of meat in the warehouse for worrying me," Emil grumbles in warning, one that I heed because with Emiliano Calvano, there is no such thing as an idle threat.

"Understood, Don Calvano."

"Good. And Camil?" I turn the laptop in her direction. She turns her smokey eyes to the screen and stares back at Emil with a mixture of sibling love and respect for her don. "I hope you enjoy your vacation because you will be lucky if I allow you out of Italy again." His words are thick with menace and have Camil shrinking back in her seat. I'm about to rail Emil for speaking to my flower in such a way, but my temper cools with his following words. "We've missed you around here. Be safe, *Sorella* (sister)."

"*Amo tuo, Fratello* (I love you, brother)," she returns with tears in her eyes.

"*Sempre* (always)." Emil ends the call, and Camil turns back to staring out the window, guilt heavy on her shoulders, and while my natural instinct is to help unburden her, I know that this is one boulder she has to carry herself.

Still, it doesn't stop me from packing up my laptop and pulling Camil into my arms to settle in for the long flight to Texas.

Texas. Just a jump from Mexico and that fateful day that changed my life forever.

20

Camil

Thirteen hours later, Boian, Dom, Lorenzo, and I step onto the tarmac of Love Field airport in Dallas, Texas, and I'm in awe at the temperature difference. Greta would joke about Texas weather being bipolar, and come to find out, she wasn't joking. It's late February, yet a warm breeze lifts my hair as we walk across the sunbaked tarmac, a bright blue, cloudless sky stretching as far as the eye can see.

I stop and lift my face to the sky. "This is wonderful. It's nice not to be freezing all the time."

"Don't get used to it. Tomorrow it's supposed to drop to the lower forties," Boian reports and laughs when I gape at him in surprise.

"Are you serious? That's like, what, a forty-degree drop?"

He spreads his arms wide and grins. "Welcome to Texas, little lady." His attempt at a southern accent is so horrific that we all burst into laughter, and it feels good to laugh––even if our lives are in danger.

We load our bags in the back of the waiting SUV, and I can't help but be disappointed by the choice of vehicle. "You couldn't have gotten us a truck?" I grouse, and the guys laugh, but I don't see what's so funny. I cross my arms over my chest. "I'm serious. If we're going to be here for an extended period, I want to get the full Texas experience."

Dom clutches his hand over his heart. "Way to stereotype, Camil," he teases from his spot in the front passenger seat.

My nose crinkles, and my stomach sours with shame. "I didn't mean to," I mumble.

"Shut the fuck up, Dom." Boian catches my eyes in the review mirror. "Don't listen to him, *fiore*. I spent time off and on here and can attest that they do love their trucks. They're just more common in the rural areas where there's more open land, farms, and livestock. Actually," he scratches at his beard, reminding me of the old spaghetti westerns I used to watch when I was a little girl, "I drove one while I was stationed here for almost a year, but we would never fit with these big goons. Even in a 250." He chuckles, and my shame from earlier melts away.

"See!" I kick the back of Dom's chair, barely budging the brute. "I'm not stereotyping."

Dom shakes his head. "Settle down little bit. I'm only teasing you."

I wave off his words and watch the scenery through the blacked-out window. Once we've been driving for nearly twenty minutes, I ask, "Where are we staying?"

"I have a house in Westlake. I also bought the bordering vacant plots to ensure the surrounding trees weren't cut down. The house isn't new but secure and can't be seen from the road with all the surrounding woodlands."

He bought a house and land?

"Why were you stationed in Texas?"

Boian seems to battle with how much he wants to divulge before finally answering, "We had work here."

But I refuse to accept his evasive answer, "We, as in...?" I probe.

Again, he hesitates before saying, "Military bullshit." That's it. No further explanation or detail––not that I expected anything. That part of Boian's life remains off-limits even to Emil. Still, it hurts that he doesn't trust me enough to open up about what happened during his extended time in the service.

"So, you and Emil stayed in Texas, or just you?"

"Me and my team."

I'm pushing my luck with my impromptu inquisition, but the tension inside the vehicle doesn't stop me from pressing forward. "Emil wasn't on your team?"

"Camil, maybe you should––"

"No, Camil. Emiliano wasn't on this team and had been out of the military for a couple of years by then."

Finally! I cheer silently.

"So, it was during your extended service?"

Boian white-knuckles the steering wheel and grumbles, "Yes, Camil. Now, can we end the interrogation already?"

"Excuse me for wanting to learn more about you," I throw back and slump down my seat.

"You know everything you need to know, Camil. Everything else is..."

"Yes?"

"Inconsequential."

I roll my eyes and return to watching the world go by outside my armored fortress. "Whatever you say, Bo."

21

Camil

I'm not sure how long we drive before we exit the highway and take the frontage road that leads to a metal guard rail with a sign that reads, "Dead End."

"Uh, I think you have missed a turn, Bo." I swivel around to look behind us for an opening when I'm jostled from side to side. Boian jumps the curb and drives across an open field until we come upon a massive oak tree. Its surrounding woodlands are so thick it's fit to be an enchanted forest from a child's fairy tale book. If the princess was being thrown around the back of a murdered-out armored SUV, that is.

Boian dodges the grand oak and navigates the SUV around smaller trees and brush until he stops in a small clearing, turns, then backs up and parks behind a fallen tree covered in budding growth. We pile out of the SUV; the guys grab our bags, and I follow them to a thicket of smaller trees and shrubs where two utility vehicles are hidden behind a tangled mess of limbs.

I let out a squeal of childlike joy at the beautiful machines. Both vehicles are solid black, with the exception of the green hood plaque with a yellow deer on it and covered in camo netting.

"This is so cool!" I rejoice and practically skip to the one in front.

Boian and the guys laugh at my merriment, but I don't care because, besides my brief stay in Romania, I have never been outside of Italy, and if Emil holds true to his threat, I may never again. So, I'm going to enjoy the taste of rural living while I can.

"I'm glad you like them, *fiore.*" Boian sets our bags in the back of the small vehicle, with Dom and Lorenzo following behind us. Boian starts up the utility vehicle and takes off like a bullet leaving Dom and Lorenzo cursing and racing to catch up. Still, where the guys are skilled drivers when it comes to road vehicles, it's clear Boian has the added benefit of being trained for all-terrain. Dom and Lorenzo pick up speed, and I hold my hair back as I look behind me to catch the shit-eating grins spread across their face as they bring their bumper a hairsbreadth from ours.

"Oh, shit. They're about to tag us, Bo!" I yell over the whipping, then squeal with excitement when Boian takes a sharp left turn, cutting the guys off and forcing them to slam on the brakes.

"Not today, baby!" Boian yells back and flips Lorenzo and Dom the bird before slowing us down to a leisurely pace.

I frantically brush away the ratted nest of hair from my face and laugh. "Oh my God, that was the most fun I have ever had!"

Boian beams at me from the driver's seat. "It doesn't take much to make you happy, does it?" and that smile——that look of utter joy on his perfectly imperfect face——is everything. It's my light in this dark world we live in, and he is my guide to navigating it.

I tell him as much when I wrap my arms around his muscular biceps and lean my head against his shoulder. "*You* make me happy." I'm not sure he heard me until he kisses my head, silently reciprocating.

Too soon, we pull through the dense woods where a white house with gray trim sits. The exterior could use a coat of paint, but other than that, it's perfect.

The guys pull up a second later and roll their eyes when I pump my fist in the air. "We'll meet in the war room in an hour," Lorenzo says before he and Dom make their way to the back of the house.

I watch them walk toward the back of the house. "Where are they going?" I ask in confusion.

Boian smiles and takes my hand. "You'll see."

I'm scanning the area and smiling like a loon when we reach the front door—— the front door with no doorknob. With a furrowed brow, I run my hands over the door to find it cold and solid as steel, then jump back when there's a loud beep, and it suddenly opens. "What did I do?" I ask the door as though it will answer back.

"You didn't do anything." I turn to Boian, who wiggles his fingers at me. "I did." He places them against the glass of one of the small windows on either side of the door. My mouth drops open in amazement when the glass lights up with a green glow around his digits, and the door swings shut. He does it again, the door beeps, gears whirl, and the door opens.

"That is amazing!" I approach the glass and run my fingers over where he just laid his fingers. "There's not a single print left behind. How is that possible?"

He shrugs. "It's a bunch of technical shit even I don't understand. You'll have to ask Lorenzo. He's the one that commissioned the work from MHS." He guides me through the open door, then shuts it behind us and locks it again.

"MHS?" I ask.

"Marron House Security," he returns, and when I don't recognize the name, he continues, "Remember Xander Cain?"

How could I forget?

I narrow my gaze on him. "I didn't exactly get a chance to meet him," I clip at the reminder of how Boian drugged me to get me on a plane to Switzerland, "but I know he was there to help find Greta. Oh, and what else did he do?" I tap a finger against my chin in mock contemplation, then snap. "That's right. He's the one that came up with the concoction that you used to knock me out and scurry me away to Switzerland."

"Right," he confirms without a scruple of remorse and continues explaining. "He's the head tech guy for MHS, and his skills rival Lorenzo's regarding security, hacking, and all things geek. He and Lorenzo put their big brains together to ensure this place is protected with MHS's latest security system. It's better protected than the crown jewels."

I decide to drop my animosity for the cyber geek for now. Still, I ask, "And you trust him?"

"And I trust him," Boian repeats, then takes a threatening step toward me with a gleam of wicked heat in his violet eyes. He doesn't stop pursuing me until my back hits the wall and my hands lift to his chest. Whether it's to push him away or pull him to me, I don't know because while the reminder of him drugging me pricks at my nerves, the weight of his body pressed against mine soothes the irritation along with his following declaration. "I would never bring you to a place without assuring it's safe first. You are more valuable than any jewel or gemstone, *mia fiore*." He brushed a lock of hair behind my ear. "You are priceless," he finishes with a gentle stroke of my cheek, and I melt into his touch, my eyelashes fluttering shut as I inhale his smell of leather and sandalwood.

"You can't say things like that, Boian," I whisper.

"Why not?" His lips brush over mine, and my eyes slide open to lock with his. They glow with possession and need, and my body immediately responds to that look. My nipples harden painfully beneath my sweater, my clit tingles, and my panties dampen with my desire.

I swallow around the desert in my mouth. "Because it confuses me."

"What about this," he presses his erection against my stomach, "is confusing, Camil?" His lips drag across mine, then down over my neck, to my collarbone, where he pulls the collar of my sweater down to get at the mounds of my breasts.

Goosebumps race across my skin with the erotic burn of his beard scraping across my soft flesh, eliciting a torrent of desire to drench my panties. I spear my fingers through his hair and tilt my hips to press harder against his solid steel cock. "What am I to you, Boian Greco? An itch to scratch? A plaything while we hide away?"

His beard sears my skin as he slides his tongue over my neck and collarbone, but I couldn't care less because, with each sting of his whiskers, he's there to soothe it away with a gentle kiss and the sweep of his tongue. I arch into his mouth and moan when he bites the plump mound of one breast.

He's breathless when he lifts his lips to hover over mine. "You are everything, Camil Radu." He slams his mouth down on mine, and the next thing I know, our clothes are off, and he's lifting me against the wall. My legs instinctively wrap around his narrow waist, and I grind my pussy against his stiff cock. "God, Camil, you will be the death of me." He follows his words with a tip of his hips, and then in one thrust, he's buried inside my pussy so deep I wince when he bumps against my cervix. "Okay?" he breathes against my face but doesn't slow his assault on my pussy. I nod frantically and pull him closer with my legs. That's all the encouragement he needs to pull out then plunge back in with such force that my back slides up the wall. With a bruising hold on my hips, he slams me down on his thick cock while he thrusts upward at a cruel pace.

We're wild, savage, and completely out of control as we fuck each other against the textured wall that rips at my skin. Still, the pain only spurs me on as I claw at Boian's back while he growls and leaves his mark on my hips with his unyielding grip, and when Boian takes my taut nipple into his mouth and bites down painfully, my pussy clenches around him, and I can feel the orgasm building to fever pitch.

Boian brings his forefinger to my mouth and presses it against my lips. "Suck. Suck it like it's my cock, baby," he orders, and I obey. I suck on his thick digit like it's his cock, and I'm starved for his cum. He pops his finger free, and I whimper in protest, then groan in wanton euphoria when he brings the same finger to my dark hole and buries it to the knuckle. It burns as it stretches me, and I buck in his hold as he thrusts his thick digit inside my ass with quick, shallow pumps. "My flower likes my finger in her ass, doesn't she? Because you're my dirty little whore." He hisses when the walls of my pussy tighten around his length. His thrusts stutter, but he doesn't stop his brutal pace. "Say it. Say you're my dirty little whore."

My moans turn to whimpers and cries of need when he slows the thrust of his hips when I don't answer him. "Bo, please..."

"Say it, Camil, then fucking beg me to make you come." His voice has turned inhuman with lust, and while the feminist in me wants to buck against him for his degrading words, the sex-crazed woman in me thrills at his dirty words.

In the end, crazed wins out, and with another whimper, I do as I'm bid. "I'm your dirty little whore. Oh, God!" I breathe when he hits my G-spot with a brutal thrust.

"What else!" he shouts and trembles with the energy it's costing him to keep himself from coming.

"I beg you, make me come," I beg, then take it up a notch and add, "Please, sir." I'm not sure where it comes from or why it sends a bolt of electricity to my already electrified core, but right now, I don't care because when I don't think he can fuck me any harder, that one simple sir releases the beast I hear in Boian's voice.

With an animalist growl, he fists my hair, making me cry out while my pussy convulses around him, and he snarls, "Come, Camil. Fucking, come!"

And I do.

I scream into the room as I milk his cock with each spasm of my pussy. Tears coat my cheeks as bone-wracking waves of pleasure crash over me. I cling to Boian as I convulse in his merciless embrace, my face buried in his neck. His fists tighten in my hair, and he thrusts twice more before fully seating himself inside me and roaring to the ceiling as his seed floods my canal. We're both breathless and drenched in sweat but refuse to pull away from each other.

We stay like that until our breathing steadies and our skin cools. Boian shivers against me and presses his face into my hair. "You are everything," he repeats, and I snuggle closer to him as tears tip over my lashes for an entirely different reason than the ones shed during my orgasmic bliss. Boian pets my hair. "Shh, baby. Don't cry." He tries to pull away to look at me, but I refuse to budge. With a sigh, he grips my ass, and then he's walking. I lift my heavy head from its hiding place when he descends a set of stairs I didn't notice before.

My head swings on a swivel as I take in the home formally thought as a single story only to find it is, in fact, a two-story and stunning. The outside might look worn and need updating, but the inside looks like it went through recent renovations with its light wood flooring, a kitchen equipped with new appliances, and gleaming quartz countertops. Everything is white except for the various robin's egg blue L-shaped sofas and natural dark wood tables.

As we walk by floor-to-ceiling windows, I glimpse an outdoor oasis with a second-floor deck, large mature trees, and a small guest house tucked between two towering oaks.

"That's where the guys are staying," Boian answers my question from earlier.

"Your home is lovely," I say in awe as he continues to carry me into what I can only suspect is the master bedroom, where a king-sized blue upholstered sleigh bed dominates the room, each side with its own side table crafted in the same dark wood as the other furnishings.

"It'll do," he jokes and gets a slap on the shoulder from me. He laughs and squeezes my ass cheeks tighter. "Come on, flower. We need to get cleaned up before the guys get back."

I pout and tighten my legs around his waist. "Fine. But just so you know, I'm not letting go."

He brushes a lock of hair from my face, and his eyes soften before he places his forehead on mine. "Promise?"

141

22

Boian

Something is happening inside me. Something that scares the shit out of me. I've always cared for Camil--never denied it--but this is the first time I wanted to say screw it and bare myself completely. Tell her about the shit that went down during my time in the service. About what happened in Mexico that constructed this wall between me and everyone else. Confess those three words to her, but I have a job to do. My priority is keeping her safe, not dropping to my knees and verbally vomiting everything I've kept locked in a steel cage. Besides, what would happen if I did tell her what I did in Mexico? A part of me knows Camil won't see me differently, and that's the problem. If I lay myself out for her to see *everything*, and she still looks at me with that look, that look of devotion, desire, and ... love, then the chains holding back the beast inside me will dissolve, and eventually, he will smother Camil's light with his filthy shadow.

No, I can't... *won't* do that to my flower.

I shut off the shower and grab one of the towels warming on the rack, and rough dry my hair, then run a hand through it for my typical perfectly messy style or, as Camil calls it, my I-don't-give-a-fuck style. I need a haircut, so I pull the shears from the mirror cabinet before slipping on some gym shorts, a white T-shirt, and running shoes. When I enter the room Camil and I will be sharing––a fact Camil has not been made aware of yet––she's just slipped on some blue jean Bermuda shorts with lace patches in various spots and a green ribbed tank top. Her feet are clad in a pair of matching green Vans and a Roma tribal anklet with small diamonds made to look like lily blooms set in a sterling silver chain—the anklet I gave her on her twenty-first birthday.

"You still have it." I gesture to the anklet.

Camil looks down and wiggles her ankle, eliciting a melodic tinkling sound from the diamonds and small charms, then looks back up with a dumbfounded expression. "Of course I do. Why wouldn't I?"

I answer with an introverted shrug. "It's the first time I've seen it on you."

"Then you aren't paying attention," she heckles. "But seriously, the only time I don't wear it is when I wear a pants suit. The slack cuffs catch on the diamonds, so I wear them mostly in summer." She pulls her shorter ebony hair into a low ponytail, drawing more attention to her bare face. While still hypnotic, her cheekbones and gray eyes aren't as defined. Old blemish scars, barely noticeable but still there, speckle her cheeks, and tiny laugh lines crinkle at the sides of her eyes. She's more beautiful like this, barefaced and relaxed, than any other time I've laid eyes on her.

The effect is like a punch to the diaphragm. My chest is so tight that I have to rub at the spot where it aches at her beauty.

"Are you alright, Bo?" Camil asks in concern, but I can't speak through the bubbling emotions clogging my throat because her beauty––inside and out–– fists my heart, crushing the stone casing around the fragile organ.

Before I know it, my lips land on hers with a quiet whimper of need. Her hands cup the back of my neck, and her lips tip up in a smile against mine, and that's when I know she understands what I'm trying to say through this kiss. Her hands stroke the hairs at my nape, and her eyes shine bright with so much fucking love that I pull away with a gasp. My stomach floods with butterflies, and my heart thunders like a Texas summer storm.

Bringing trembling hands to her cheeks, I graze a thumb over her lips. The lips I thought to be a pale rose red are actually a dusky pink. Her smile isn't perfect, with one bottom incisor slightly overlapping the other. But those eyes––those eyes draw me in–– dark and stormy when angry and gleaming like silver when happy.

My fingers flex against her cheeks when the back of my eyes begin to sting, and my mouth floods with saliva. "Camil, I..." Nothing else comes out even though I'm mentally screaming at myself to say it. To tell her! But my mouth won't form the words.

You're a monster and will only cause her more pain. She will hate you when you tell her what you have planned, the beast booms inside my head, reminding me that I'm about to force her to marry me. Force her to marry a man she loves but who–– as far as she knows–– doesn't love her, and it may be what has her running again, and any reasonable man would let her go. Instead, she got me, and I'm not letting her go. She will hate me, but maybe it's for the best. Besides, if she hates me, it means she still loves me.

"Yes?" She floats her hands up my arms to clutch my wrists, and that gleam of hope in her eyes guts me.

I swallow, clear my throat, and drop my hands to clasp one of hers. "When the guys get here, I need you to keep an open mind and listen to *everything* I say before you go off the rails."

The sparkle of hope in her silver gaze twists into hard steel with jagged edges when she pulls her hand from mine and crosses her arms over her chest. "I'm assuming we're waiting for the guys because they're a part of whatever this is?" I nod. "Great, Bo, just ruin a perfect moment." She throws her hands up and brings them down to slap against her thighs. "I'm finally relaxed, and now I have to prepare to dig three graves for three huge-ass men after they tell me something that will piss me off." I would laugh if there were anything remotely funny about what I am about to do. "You need a haircut, by the way," Camil points out.

I run my hand through my hair with a heavy sigh and realize I must have dropped the scissors by the bathroom door when I stumbled into my Camil-induced stupor. I walk over, pluck them from the floor, and hand them to her. "My thoughts exactly. You did such a good job with yours. You think you can do mine later?"

She tips up one corner of a dark brow and takes the shears from my hand. "You sure you want me to have scissors right before you piss me off?" She twirls the shears around her finger, then catches them in her fist, pointed end facing me.

I smile, then, in one quick motion, I grab her wrist and twist it around to the small of her back. At the same time, I turn her and press her face against the wall. The hold isn't painful, more a move to subdue her, and from how her body melts into mine, I would say it's working. Her ass molds itself over my hard cock, and she grinds against me, vibrating with need.

I make sure to brush the coarse hair of my beard across her cheek when I speak into her ear. "Even if you hated me, I would trust you with my life." I bury my nose in her hair and inhale deeply. "And I need you to trust me right now." I pull away and adjust my throbbing hard-on before taking her hand. "Come, let's get this over with." Dom and Lorenzo take that moment to enter the house upstairs.

"Always a bad sign," she mumbles and turns to me with guarded eyes. Still, she takes my offered hand, and I bask in the warmth as long as I can because I have no illusions that Camil Radu will fight me when she sees the contract that will bind her to me till death do us part.

23

Camil

D read pulls in my stomach at what Bo has to tell me and the fact that he needs Lorenzo and Dom present. He's not sending me away again––he all but said so. Then what's so bad that it would set me off enough for Bo to need back-up?

We ascend the stairs into the main living area, where Dom and Lorenzo stand with looks of apprehension on their handsome faces, but it's the fact that neither will meet my eyes that has my back up.

Lorenzo hands Bo a manila envelope and pen. "Let's sit." Bo gently nudges me to the robin's egg blue L-shaped couch and sits beside me before pulling a single sheet of parchment paper from the envelope. "You're a member of the Calvano Roma *famiglia*, but only by association."

My blood sizzles in my veins at the backhanded compliment. "What do you mean 'by association'? I am more than––"

"This," he holds up the document as though I didn't speak, "will make it official. I don't have Calvano blood, but as Emiliano's second, I'm recognized as a made man, and by proxy, it makes you off limits." Boian extends the paper and gestures for me to take it when I stare down at it like a viper waiting to strike. "Camil." I startle at my name and take the paper with a trembling hand because I know what I'm about to see. Sure enough, when I look down, I see mine and Boian's names printed clearly at the bottom with the words CERTIFICATE OF MARRIAGE in big, bold filagree at the top. There's a signature below Boian's printed name but none beneath mine.

At least the bastard has the courtesy not to forge my signature.

Taking a steadying breath, I force myself to remain calm and formulate my thoughts into words instead of flying into a rage. However, I'm finding it difficult to think rationally around the acidic anger blistering me from the inside out.

With another deep inhale and exhale, I release the tension in my shoulders and say, "You want me to marry you." It's not a question, but Boian answers anyway.

He enters my personal space and hovers over me with his towering height and intimidating brawn, but I refuse to cower. "You *will* marry me, Camil, because it's the best way to keep you safe. There will always be danger in our world, and you're a potential target, but this marriage will put you in a class that tells our enemies not to fuck with you, or they will have the whole of the Calvano Roma coming for their heads."

I tilt my head to the side and look at him with skepticism. "What about Greta? Emil made a show of her being under his protection, and someone still took her."

Boian shakes his head. "Greta and Emil weren't married, so she didn't have the protection of the *famiglia* name."

I look back and forth between the three hulking men and would laugh at the way Dom and Lorenzo fidget where they stand if I wasn't already barely keeping my temper at bay. "So, you want to marry me to protect me? You want me to sign away my freedom on the off chance that a *name* will keep our enemies from using me as bait or kill me for revenge?" I ask to clarify.

Boian's hands fist at his sides, and his jaw ticks before he answers, "Yes," between clenched teeth.

I've loved Boian since the moment I met him, and even as a young girl, my heart would pound with excitement whenever he entered the room and ache with sadness when he left.

"Not because you're in love with me?" I lay the question at his feet and watch without sympathy as he battles to find the right words, but if they're anything but the three words I have wanted to hear from this man since I was a child, then I'm not interested.

So, when Boian speaks again, the younger Camil's fantasy of the violet-eyed beast saving the captured princess and confessing that she's the love of his life crumbles. "For God's sake, Camil! I care enough about you to want to protect you. Isn't that enough?"

149

He leaps to his feet and faces Lorenzo and Dom, who have remained silent the entire time.

Is that enough?

The hot-tempered Italian in me says, "Hell no," but then the part of me that rarely shows itself––the sensible part––says to let go of this foolish quest for Boian's heart. If he insists on being trapped in a cage of his own making, then who am I to try and free him? One thing is for sure. I'll be damned if he traps me along with him.

Resolved in my decision, I stand with the marriage certificate in hand and make sure to make eye contact with each man before declaring, "You and your savior complex can go to hell." I rip the parchment in half, then quarters, before tossing the scraps in Boian's face. The scraps of paper flutter to the ground like my dreams of marrying the man I love and who loves me back.

Boian sighs and opens the drawer of a small accent table next to the door. My eyes narrow when he retrieves another manila folder, then pulls out another copy of the marriage certificate. "You don't think I have multiple copies? You can tear up hundreds of these, Camil, and there will still be a hundred more."

My fists clench at my side, and my throat grows thick with impending tears. "Then save us both the trouble by gathering every copy and torching them because I will never sign it," I choke on my words and turn away from him.

"Dammit, Camil! Get the idea of living a fucking fairy tale life out of your head. That is not the world we live in. No matter how far you try to run," he growls his last statement, and I wince at the resentful comment.

"I may not be able to run from this world, but it doesn't mean I have to marry you," I argue and turn back to him when my eyes have cleared.

Boian throws open his arms. "It's either me or someone else in the family, baby. Either way, the marriage won't be about love but rather about securing alliances and pumping out heirs. At least with me, you get the devil, you know." His words are cruel and meant to push me away... and it's working. When I don't respond to his outburst, his nostrils flare, and his eyes turn electric. He reaches for the pen still lying on the coffee table. "I can easily forge your fucking signature, Camil, but I'm giving you the respect of talking to you first in the hope that maybe for once, you will be reasonable." I still don't speak, and his wrathful gaze searches my defeated one. "Are you really willing to risk marrying a complete asshole who won't appreciate you instead of me?" he finishes with a clenched jaw and something feral in his violet eyes. The idea of me marrying someone else wakes the beast inside him because I'm already his in Boian's mind. His possession. His plaything.

But I am neither of those things. Not anymore.

With a lift of my chin, I do my best to speak with all the confidence I can muster. "*If* I decide to marry, at least with another man, I won't have to spend my life pretending I don't love him, that I don't crave his very presence or even the barest of his touches. I can tolerate living in a loveless marriage with a stranger because then I won't be tortured by seeing him every day with the knowledge that I have given him all of me, yet he refuses to do the same." I turn for the front door but stop with my hand white-knuckling the knob. With tears stinging my eyes, I steady my breathing before looking over my shoulder to deliver the final blow. "I would rather marry for an alliance than be married to a coward." Then open the door and shut it behind me with a gentle click rather than my typical enraged slam because... why bother?

Boian Greco will protect me with his life, but he will never love me, and that's a reality I have to accept.

For now...

24

Boian

Her words cut deep. They rip through flesh, muscle, and bone all the way to the marrow. She would rather be with another man than be married to me. I expected nothing less. Still, the look in her eyes and those words on her lips crush me. There is resolution in those storm cloud-colored eyes. She isn't saying those words out of spite. She's saying them in truth, and when she walks out the door and shuts it with a soft click instead of her usual slam, I know she's done, done giving me time to come to my senses, done giving me chance after chance.

It's better this way, my inner voice laments, and I have no choice but to agree.

"What now, Boss?" Lorenzo asks to my back.

I turn with a heavy sigh and grab another copy of the marriage contract that suddenly feels like a two-ton weight in my hand at the thought of what I am about to do. However, it doesn't stop me from grabbing the pen I left for Camil and scribbling her name across the document. My gut tightens with my betrayal while my heart thrills with the knowledge that Camil is now my wife.

I hand the document to Lorenzo. "Get this to the judge, so it's official." He nods in acknowledgment, but his lips tip up in a slight snarl. He's pissed by my actions and wants to say something. Instead, he turns and walks away before my woods halt his retreat. "Disobeying a direct order will result in your dismissal from the *famiglia*––*after* you're beaten bloody. Emiliano, your don, has sanctioned this marriage and whatever it takes to make it happen." Lorenzo doesn't turn. He only nods again, then continues on his path.

"While I hate what you did," Dom speaks up, "I understand why you had to do it."

"Thank you, brother."

"Of course. Should I go find her?"

I chew my bottom lip when the unfamiliar feeling of indecision has me hesitating to answer. While a part of me wants to kick Dom in the ass and bark at him for not already being out the door and following to watch over her, the other part tells me to let her be, that she's safe on my property.

Eventually, my concern for Camil's safety pulls ahead of the pack, and I nod. "Yes, but make sure to give her space."

"*Si*, Boss."

Dom is out the door in two strides, and once I'm alone, I call Emil. "How did she take it?" he asks in the way of greeting.

"Exactly as expected. And I quote, 'I would rather marry for an alliance than a coward,'" I repeat her words and feel their stabbing pain all over again.

"I believe her." Emil chuckles and then sighs, and I picture him running a hand through his hair in irritation. "Has the certificate been sent to the judge?"

"Lorenzo is doing it now *after* I reminded him of what happens to people who disobey a direct order."

"They practically grew up with her too, Boian. Remember that. It's only natural for them to be torn between following orders and being loyal to Camil," Emil defends, and I'm so thrown by his rationality that I can't help but laugh.

"The great Emiliano Calvano is being reasonable? Where was this when you snatched your fiancée from her life and punished her for a debt she had no idea existed?" I'm only half jesting with him, and the other half, I'm fuming with him for daring to side with Lorenzo's possible disobedience on the matter.

"Fuck off. I'm well aware of my past offenses against my fiancée and will forever be in *her* debt for forgiving me. It's those failures that have me thinking reasonably. If you planned to harm Camil, I would have never sanctioned this union. As it is, I see this as the best way to protect the woman I consider a sister."

"And Greta?" I ask with a tip of my brow.

"*Mi regina* was hesitant of our plan, but with a little persuasion," he says with a salacious tone, "she's come to understand that it's a necessary evil."

"Too much information, brother."

"You sure? It sounds like you could use some tips in that department," Emil taunts.

"Get fucked. I'll call you when I have an update." I disconnect to his roaring laughter echoing over the line.

"It's been sent, and I have confirmation it's been received. Congratulations," Lorenzo grumbles insincerely.

I turn to the man with an exasperated eye roll. "Stop with the bitchy passive-aggressive comments. It's beneath you. I know you don't like how Emil and I are going about this, but what's the alternative? Say Camil marries someone else in the family." My stomach sours, and my fists clench at my side. "He will have his own home and his own guards. She won't be in a place where we can protect and watch over her." When he doesn't so much as blink at my reasoning, I pinch the bridge of my nose to ward off the impending headache. "Come on, Lorenzo, you know there's no other person more willing to lay down their life for her."

"You're wrong," he argues, and my eyes narrow on him. "I would die for her. Dom would too."

I step up to the man with an audible growl. "What are you saying, Lorenzo? Did you want to be the one to marry her? To bed her?" My tone is razor sharp, and my eyes daggers, daring him to answer wrongly.

"If my don asked me to, I would. But that's not what you're really asking, is it?" The fucker has the nerve to smirk.

"Are you in love with Camil?" I cut to the chase.

He doesn't answer for two beats before he grins widely. "I love Camil like a brother loves a sister." The breath I'm holding releases in a silent rush before

Lorenzo continues, "But at least I love her *and* am willing to tell her."

My fist flies and lands with a satisfying crunch against his jaw, then my hands are fisting his collar, and I'm shoving him against the wall. "You have no idea what I feel or why I'm doing what I'm doing. You have no idea about the things that haunt me—that would haunt Camil if I told her. Whether any of us like it or not, her safety comes before her happiness, and if you have a problem with that, then you can fuck off." I shove off him and storm out through the back door. The warm Texas breeze ruffles my hair, reminding me of the haircut I desperately need, and despite the current cluster fuck we're in, I smile when I remember Camil's words from earlier. *You sure you want me to have scissors right before you piss me off?*

I wasn't lying when I told her I trusted her with my life, and if she wanted to end it, then so be it. Because my life, my soul ... my heart, is hers.

I pace around the manicured back lawn and come upon the small fenced-in garden I kept cultivated while on assignment all those years ago. Now, the same people who come once a week to clean and check on things have begun the process of aerating and tilling the soil for re-planting.

One of the many messages I sent while in the air was informing them that I wouldn't need their services for the foreseeable future, then immediately denying them access by changing the biometrics on all the entry points. As far as they know, I'm a legitimate businessman they rarely saw but paid them well for their services and their silence. I'm sure some of them heard rumors about me, but none of them asked questions, which earned them a hefty holiday bonus every Christmas.

I drop my ass to the wooden bench beneath the aging willow tree that acts as a source of shade in the hot summer months. I replay the fight between Camil and me and curse myself for the brutish way I went about it. I was doing well until she started questioning my motives. Then, like the coward she accused me of being, I started spouting off bullshit just to push her buttons.

With a growl of self-loathing, I scrub my hands over my face as though I can erase the exhaustion of the past few weeks. Between sleeping on the couch during our time in the cabin and the nightmares that clawed at my brain every night, I only sleep a couple of hours at a time. I am used to not getting much sleep but add in the back and forth between Camil and me and the stress of the unknown threat that haunts us, lying and waiting for us to fuck up, and I can't help but feel the exhaustion weighing down on me like a Texas longhorn sitting on my chest.

Camil may hate me right now, but that comes second to finding the shadow that is stalking Camil and exterminating them or risk them making a move to snuff out *mia fiore's* light.

25

Camil

"You may hate me for saying so, but I'm going to say it anyway," Dom warns when he approaches to pace beside me. "I agree with Boian. I think this is the best way to keep you safe." Dom has never pulled any punches with me, and I appreciate that he isn't doing it now, even if he's siding with the man currently enemy number one. Maybe that's a bit dramatic, but I stand by it.

I sigh and pivot to walk the other way on the tall stone wall that borders one side of Boian's home. "I don't hate you. In fact, I agree with you. I know what it means to officially be part of the *famiglia*."

"Then what's the problem?" Dom asks.

I roll my eyes. *Boys can be so stupid sometimes.* "I love him, Dom. I've loved him since I was a little girl, and he carried me to get my knee looked at after I fell." I abruptly spin around, nearly giving Dom a heart attack before my heels fall back to the stone, and I walk back the way I came.

"I get that, Camil, but would you honestly rather marry a man who only married you to get ahead or a man that actually gives a damn about you? One that will lay down his life for you—"

"I don't want anyone laying down their life for me," I grumble and jump to the ground before stomping away with Dom on my heels.

"Too bad, Camil. Because you have me, Lorenzo, Boian, and Emil, who won't hesitate to jump in front of a bullet for you." Dom's calloused hand clutches my forearm and swings me around to face him. Unexpectedly my lungs compress under what feels like the weight of an elephant sitting on my chest, and the dam holding back my emotions breaks when my eyes meet Dom's, which shine with unwavering devotion.

My face scrunches in an ugly cry, and my fists pummel his thickly muscled chest as tears fall like rivers down my cheeks. The tears are for the truth in his words because these men are my family, and I will willingly give my life for theirs as quickly as they would give theirs for mine. The punches are my anger at our world for taking a bullet even being a possibility. I cry silently as my fists beat against Dom's brawny chest while he stands steadfast as my willing punching bag. The more I hit, the more I cry for the life I could have had if I hadn't been born into a world of blood and tears. Then I cry harder at the thought of what it would mean if I hadn't been born into this world, to lose the people I call family. So many warring emotions make for a tsunami of confusion in my head while my heart screams at me because it knows exactly where it belongs. That's why I don't stop until my punches weaken and my tears start to dry.

When my biceps burn with exertion, I drop my arms, and Dom drags me into his chest, wraps his arms around me, and whispers words of brotherly affection in my ear.

He rocks me in his arms until I mumble into his chest, "I'm going to marry Boian Greco."

"I know you are." He lifts my head from his chest and smiles down at me. "And you," he taps the end of my nose, "are going to live happily ever after."

I bat his hand away and poke a finger in his side, exploiting the big man's weakness. And as expected, Dom yelps like a little girl and squirms out of reach. We both break out into a fit of laughter, and tears stream down my cheeks for a much more enjoyable reason this time.

"Leave it to Dom to be the one to make you laugh." Boian's attempt at levity instantaneously silences my laughter.

I swivel my head to look at him from over my shoulder. "He's not forcing me to marry him, so..." I shrug.

"Camil," Dom admonishes with a tip of a dark eyebrow.

I roll my eyes at my best friend and turn to face Boian, and it never ceases to amaze me how just looking at him makes me go weak in the knees.

The man is six-foot-three inches of sinewy muscle. He has defined cheekbones, a powerful jaw, and his otherworldly chromatic eyes with their reddish-blue hue. I've dreamt of those eyes too many nights for me to count. They are always watching me with uninhibited desire and undying love. He speaks to me through those eyes of his. He tells me how much he loves me and can never live without me and...

I shove my girly notions of fairy tales away when I feel the budding of new tears prick at my eyes. I adopt a mask of stoicism and clear the damnable emotions from my throat. "I'll do it."

Boian tucks his hands inside his jeans pockets and tips his head to the side. "Do what, exactly?"

I give him a look that, if I were the scorned Medusa, would transform Boian into a block of stone right now. I narrow my eyes at him and say with gritted teeth, "I'll sign the damn marriage certificate."

His lips stretch to a full grin, he crosses his arms over his chest, and I stand there trying and failing not to drool over the arm porn on full display. "Hmm. What changed your mind?"

I tear my eyes away from his bulging biceps and shrug. "You're as good as any other man, I suppose," I goad and get the desired effect when he bares his teeth and a violet spark ignites in his eyes.

"Good thing the paperwork has already been sent to a judge and notarized," he spits back, and my blood roils in my veins.

I'm two beats away from slinging insults, but I catch myself before I release a torrent of verbal daggers because Boian can't hide the slight quickening of his breath, the twitch of a smirk on his lips, or the prominent bulge in his pants. The asshole is goading me into a fight. He wants me to be out-of-control-Camil——because it turns him on.

Well, screw him. I'm not playing into his little game.

"I assume you forged my name and had one of your crooked judges sign off on it?" I ask emotionlessly while I'm trembling with a myriad of emotions inside.

"Of course," Boian answers with a condescending lilt, but I refuse to give in to his needling. So, we stand staring at each other, waiting for the other to crack.

"Great!" Dom's enthusiastic tone breaks through our standoff. "Now that that's settled, how about we go inside, and I'll start dinner?"

I turn my most endearing smile on him. "Only if it's steak. I hear Texans are known for their steaks."

Dom laughs heartily, throws a heavy arm over my shoulders, and guides me to the front of the house. "That one is true, but that's because they have the best cattlemen. As we speak, I've got some beautiful Nolan Ryan tenderloins marinating in my secret sauce."

"The baseball player?" I ask in surprise

"You know of him?" Dom asks with his own lilt of surprise.

"I love American sports. Though, Greta has me obsessed with hockey more than any other." We continue our conversation about sports while Boian's footfalls behind us sound like a toddler stomping around like he just got told no dessert until he eats his vegetables.

Stupid boy.

26

Boian

H er lack of fight is starting to piss me off. Camil is hot-headed on a good day. Dump all the shit I have on her, and she should be a ball of fury right now. Yet she walks away arm and arm with Dom, cool as gelato. Nothing like the Camil I know and love to battle with––a fact that has me on edge. Is she up to something? Or is she shutting down on me–– giving me a taste of my own medicine?

My hands twitch at my sides with the need to pull her to me, devour those berry-sweet lips, and bring that spark back to her silver eyes. I want, no need, to feel her come to life under my touch and beg for more. I'm a selfish bastard when it comes to her attention, but do I care? Not a single fuck.

We enter the house and go straight to the back-yard, where Lorenzo is heating up the large built-in grill. "The potatoes will be done in thirty minutes, and there's salad on the table." Lorenzo points out the large bowl of leafy greens and an array of dressings on the picnic table.

Camil giggles like a kid in a candy store and grabs an eco-friendly paper bowl to fill with salad, a mountain of shredded cheese, and way too much ranch dressing. Her eyes narrow at me when she catches my look of disgust at her ranch concoction. "Don't judge. Greta made me one like this back home, and it was good."

I shake my head. "First hockey, now ranch. That woman will make you an American by this time next year." I fill my bowl with greens and add a drizzle of balsamic dressing.

"Technically, hockey started as just a Canadian sport," she corrects me around a mouth full of salad. "And don't judge it until you try it."

Camil has become obsessed with the Texas hockey team thanks to Greta, her wardrobe gradually transforming from her usual muted pastels or black work clothes to the team's signature green.

Watching her eat and animatedly explain to Lorenzo and Dom why hockey is so great gives me an idea that may have her warming back up to me and the idea of being married to me. It's a small gesture, but Camil is never one to ask for big gifts or expensive things. I scroll through my phone while the three talk and find precisely what I'm looking for.

"What has you smiling like the cat that's caught the canary?" Lorenzo asks where he leans against the stone wall surrounding the patio.

"Maybe not a canary, but perhaps one pissed off Camil Radu."

He nudges me with his shoulder. "You mean Camil Greco."

His words hit me like a ton of bricks. Camil Greco, my wife. Fuck me, Camil is my wife. The feeling of elation from moments ago is nothing compared to the overwhelming sense of peace and happiness that washes over me like a tidal wave with the knowledge that Camil is legally and undisputedly *mine*. My grin doubles, and suddenly all the bullshit surrounding us is like vapor in the wind. Gone, if only for a moment.

"Steaks are ready!" Dom announces proudly, and Camil rushes to grab her plate.

She seizes a foil-wrapped potato and tosses it from hand to hand before dropping the piping hot side to her plate and carefully opening it. Dom drops a healthy serving of tenderloin on her plate, and I swear the woman starts to drool. Camil doesn't bother to wait for us to get our food. She says a quick prayer and then cuts into her steak like a man eating his first good meal after serving time. She places the meat on her tongue and hums around the bite, then moans like a fucking seductress when she bites into the tender meat. Dom, Lorenzo, and I freeze and stare at the siren making love to her meal.

"Damn, Camil. I'm gay, and even I'm turned on by how you're enjoying that steak." Dom laughs and adjusts himself in his jeans.

"Watch it," I growl, but he just shrugs and goes about devouring his own steak. My eyes swing to Lorenzo in warning, but he's already taking his seat. Probably to hide the erection Camil is giving us poor men.

Camil tips her head curiously at me, and I wait for the glib remark I know dances on the tip of her tongue. And my wife doesn't disappoint. "Wait, so we're not allowed to take a lover?"

I choke on my bite of meat while struggling to control the need to strangle her. I know she's trying to rile me up, and she's succeeded because the only one who can ever make me lose my shit is Camil.

When I finally swallow the chunk of steak, I turn thundering eyes to her. "I don't find that fucking funny, Camil. But if you need it spelled out for you, then fine." I lean across the table and pin her with a deadly stare. "If any man *or* woman touches you in a manner even remotely close to sexual or romantic, they will be strung up in the warehouse, their screams of mercy so loud that all of Rome will hear them. Does that answer your question?" I end with a clench of my teeth and nearly flip the fucking table when Camil rolls her eyes and stuffs another piece of meat in her mouth.

"Don't be so damn dramatic. I'm messing with you, Bo." Bo, not Boian, not asshole. I plop down with an exasperated huff and grip the roots of my hair. "You're right." I look back at her. She points at my head with her fork. "You need a haircut. When we're done, I'll cut it."

And that's it. No fighting, and no more egging me on. Camil got her barb in and got the exact reaction she was looking for—the proof that I cared a lot more than I let on. And I fell for it.

I chuckle and run a hand over my beard. "Well played, *fiore.*"

Camil flashes me a wicked grin. "I have no idea what you're talking about." She plays innocent, then returns to enjoying her meal with a saucy wink meant just for me.

We eat in comfortable silence, one of us slotting in a funny quip or Camil asking me a question about my time in Texas, and I expect the three massive men to gorge themselves. What I don't expect is for Camil to eat her weight in steak alongside us. The woman never ceases to amaze me or turn me on. Even now, slumped in her chair, holding her full belly, she looks magnificent.

"I am going to be sick later, but it was so worth it." She sighs as she takes in the manicured lawn and small, freshly prepared garden, but it's the old willow with the bench set beneath it that has her eyes twinkling like stars on a cloudless night. "I love that tree. It's like something from an enchanted forest," she says dreamily, and suddenly I envision a little girl with Camil's dark curls and my unusual eyes, giggling and skipping around the tree. At the same time, Camil sits watching our daughter, her stomach swollen with our son. The scene would knock me on my ass if I weren't already sitting. As it is, I'm off balance and have to grip the armrest of my chair and take slow, steady breaths to calm my galloping heart.

I never thought about my future because it was a waste of time. In the mafia, you were lucky to see your child be born, let alone see them grow into adulthood, but now my future is all I can think about. Camil loves kids. Therefore, they have always been in her future, and it sends an odd rush of tranquility through me––even when a part of me believes I should be fucking terrified. I suppose the reason I'm not is because with Camil as their mother, even if I fail as a father, our children will never want for love. Plus, Camil will kick my ass before she allows me the option of failure. I chuckle at the vision of a pregnant Camil waddling after me in a rage.

"What's so funny?" Camil poses with a dark brow tipped up in suspicion.

"Nothing, *fiore.*"

"Uh-huh," she says but doesn't probe, and I'm glad for it because no matter how much I relished the idea of Camil and me having a family... I'm just not sure I can give it to her because if there's one thing that's for sure is that ours is a cruel world.

27

Camil

Never in my life have I had to act so unaffected by Boian Greco.

I have always been open with my feelings and desire for him, so standing behind him, his silky black locks between my fingers, pretending that I don't want to grip those strands in my hands while I ride him like a show pony, is torture. Every time I catch myself picturing him between my legs, watching his thick girth disappear into my tight canal as he shoves himself deep inside me, I have to mentally reprimand myself and focus on a silent breath to re-center my thoughts, only for the fantasy to return when he catches my eyes in the mirror above the sink. In that moment, I can almost feel the bite of pain of his intrusion, increasing the erotic pleasure of being taken by my beast... my husband. I shiver at that word. After all these years, I finally have the man of my dreams, yet I have nothing without Boian's heart—a fact I have to come to live with.

I pull the long strands until a good half an inch is exposed, then cut and watch them fall to Boian's towel-covered shoulders. Shoulders I long to sink my teeth into to muffle my screams of climax.

A shiver runs through me, and Boian doesn't miss the goosebumps that crawl across my skin. "Something wrong, *fiore*?" he asks with a knowing smirk and a look of mischief, staring back at me in the reflection of the master bathroom mirror.

I straighten my shoulders and continue to cut. "I think that cold front is coming in sooner than we thought. There's a chill in the air."

The bastard laughs and catches my eyes in the mirror. "You've never been a liar, Camil. In fact, you're brutally honest. Why start lying now?"

His words get my back up, and without thinking, I blurt, "Because I have no choice now," and then go about my work.

But the grooming secession is cut short when a steel band latches around my waist, and like a contortionist, Boian swings me around to his front, where he plants me on his lap. He lifts my chin with rough fingers, his eyes an icy violet. "Don't *ever* lie to me, Camil Greco. Our marriage may not be the fairy tale you wished for, but we have always been honest with one another——"

"Don't you fucking dare lecture me about honesty, Boian Greco. A lie of omission is still a lie."

His brow furrows, and my weaker side wants to run my thumb over that spot to soothe him. "If I've kept something from you, it was for your own good."

171

Those words are a match to a barrel of gunpowder. My hands dive into his hair and grip the roots painfully. If the wince on Boian's face is any indicator, then violently yank his head back. His face is tilted to the ceiling, but his eyes look down at me through dark lashes.

"Who's the liar now?" I tighten my grip, and he growls in response. "You say it's for my own protection, but I think... I *know* the real reason is that you're too afraid to share yourself with anyone. Even me." My voice wobbles with defeat and soul-crushing sadness, angering me further. My hands grip his roots to the point that my knuckles turn white, and I can feel his heartbeat through his scalp. My bottom lip quivers, and I don't realize I'm crying until Boian wipes a tear from my cheek.

I release his hair and move to stand, but Boian grabs my wrist in one hand and then swings one of my legs over his hip. I'm straddling him now, his erection pressing against my ass.

I want to hide in my room. I want to cry and scream into my pillow, but my heart begs to cuddle up to my husband and be in this moment with him. So, I don't fight him when he lifts my trembling chin to bring us eye to eye.

"You're right," he says, shocking me with his admission. I wipe a hand under my nose, and he smiles at my unladylike actions. He leans to the side to grab a box of tissues, and I take one with a thankful smile.

"I am?" I sniffle and blow my nose.

Boian smooths a piece of my hair behind my ear, then grazes my earlobe between his thumb and forefinger. It's not sexual but rather something he does absentmindedly.

"You are." He pauses, and I watch as he wars with himself.

I hold my breath and silently beg him to open himself up to me until I can't stand it anymore and lift my hands to cup his bearded cheeks to make sure his violet eyes are focused on mine. "Nothing you tell me will make me think poorly of you." He opens his mouth to argue, but I shake my head in warning. "*Nothing*," I stress, and his eyes study my face for so long I think he will ignore my words and freeze me out again.

But he surprises me when he nods and says, "I killed a woman and her children."

I keep my features schooled even as my stomach drops and my throat tightens at his confession. I know Boian has done––and still does––terrible things, but I could never imagine he would hurt, let alone *kill*, a mother and her children. No, there has to be a reasonable explanation.

I drop my hands to his shoulders and massage the tense muscles there. "Explain," I demand softly.

He releases a breath with a puff of his cheeks. "We had a mission in Sinaloa, Mexico. A cartel leader was selling women and children, and we were sent to blow the compound to shit and exterminate the bastard that ran it. And we were successful––only..." Boian stops suddenly, and his eyes turn haunted before clenching shut, but I refuse to let him hide.

I glide my finger over the bridge of his nose. "Hey, open your eyes." His eyes lids flutter open and tortured violet orbs look back at me. "Keep going. I'm right here."

His hands on my hips tighten as though testing my words before he gathers himself to continue. "I was having trouble with my equipment. I couldn't get a good heat signature reading, but my captain insisted that the count was right and everyone was out, so I pressed the detonator and watched the compound explode in hellfire. It wasn't until later that evening that I was informed that the cartel leader's wife and kids had been unexpectedly brought to the compound." I know what he's going to say before he says it, but still, his words are like a knife to the heart. "They were inside, Camil. Two innocent children and a woman so beaten down by her bastard husband that she didn't have the strength or means to leave him. I," he beats a fist against his chest, "killed them, Camil."

He tries to stand this time, but I tighten my grip on his shoulders, and my legs curl around his waist and lock around the chair. "No, you're not running from this––running from me. You're going to listen to me now. That woman and her children died because of your actions," Boian cringes in self-disgust, and it filets my heart further, but I continue, "but you did not intentionally kill them. You trusted your captain and your team to do their jobs, and they failed you, so I can see why it's so hard to trust anyone. But Boian," I lift his head again and wait for him to open his eyes and look at me. When he does, I can't help the tears that clog my throat at the look of desperation in his eyes. He's desperate for forgiveness, but the people he needs it from are gone, so I take on the mantle of being their proxy, "you are not some heartless killer. You feel remorse, and I can see the torment and disgust you carry for yourself. A heartless, *unredeemable* murderer would shrug it off and move on to their next kill. You have carried this around like a boulder chained to your neck. It's time to forgive yourself because if there is one thing I can be certain of, it's that that woman and her children are dancing in heaven, free from the terror of living with a man willing to sell innocent people into sexual slavery." I feel completely drained when I'm done with my speech. The only thing keeping me from collapsing against Boian's chest is the look of awe––and something else that makes my heart race––in his eyes.

He pulls me into his chest, his eyes volleying between mine. The smile that tips his lips is like a blast of oxygen to my lungs, only for it to be stolen when he slams his lips to mine and drinks like a man lost in the desert who's finally getting his first sip of water. I let him gorge on my lips while I bask in the beat of his heart beneath my hand on his chest and the peace of forgiveness that warms the air around him.

I smile when his kiss becomes clumsy as he tries to hold back his elation. I want to laugh and squeeze him tight but I refuse to interrupt this kiss.

Instead, Boian does it for me when he whispers, "I love you, Camil Radu."

My lungs lock up, and my heart stops before starting again at the speed of a formula one race car. Boian laughs and refuses to allow me to pull away to ensure I heard him correctly. I push harder and bite his lip, only making him laugh more.

I take advantage, pull my lips away from his, and stare wide-eyed at the man before me. "What did you just say?"

He smirks and squeezes my ass. "You heard me."

My eyes narrow in a warning. "Say it again."

Boian's smile drops, and his eyes turn severe but not harsh. "I love you, Camil Radu, and if you let me, I'll spend the rest of my life making up for not telling you sooner."

I fist his collar and yank him toward me so we're nose to nose. "My name is Camil Greco, and there is nothing to make up for because I love you too, and love doesn't keep records of wrongs." And I seal my words with a kiss.

28

Boian

The following days are like a dream. Scratch that. They're like my dirtiest fantasies come to life. Camil and I spend our nights––and days––in bed, either fucking like we hate each other or making love, something I thought my black heart would never experience. And Jesus, the woman is unquenchable, barely giving my dick enough time to recover before straddling my lap and riding me into the sunset. My dick is sore, but all she has to do is flash that wicked grin, and I have her bent over the nearest object, taking her with a brutality that makes her moan and scream like she's paid to do so.

Like now, for example. I have her pressed against the banister as I redden her ass with a wooden spatula. "What did I say about going outside by yourself?" I grit and bring the spatula down on her ass. One of the last spots on her ass still a creamy olive tone, turns pink, and she thrusts her ass out, begging for more.

"It was just a walk to the mailbox," she whines, then gasps when I land another swat to a spot already colored with the imprint of the spatula.

"And where is the mailbox, Camil?" I'm so turned on as she moans and begs for more punishment that I can hammer nails with my cock, but the fear gnawing at my chest and the anger for her putting herself at risk still pulses through my veins.

My heart stopped when I found her gone from where I had left her on the couch, napping. It hadn't taken me long to check my men's progress in finding who was following her back in Romania, which added up to a big, fat, fucking nothing. The lack of information put me in a less-than-pleasant mood, which deteriorated further when I returned to find the couch empty.

"B... by the road," she stutters, squeezing her legs together. One detail I've discovered about Camil is that my girl is a whore for pain and can come just from a good flogging alone. A fact that makes my already sore cock ache more.

"By." *Smack.* "The." *Smack.* "Road," I finish, then drop the spatula when I see her juices wetting her thighs.

"I'm sorry... Oh God, Boian, please. I need to come!"

My flower doesn't need to ask twice. I pull my jeans down just enough to free my cock, then shove myself inside her tight heat to the hilt. Her pussy sheaths me like a fist, and I groan as she instantly spasms around me, the echoes of her cry of release the sweetest of songs. She slumps against the banister when her orgasm finally wanes, but I don't allow her the option to rest. I fist her disheveled hair and yank her back by the roots. Her back arches against my chest, and her breasts thrust forward. I palm the plump globes and pinch the tender peaks of her nipples, and growl, "Fuck me, *Fiore*. Bounce on my cock while I watch your pussy swallow me whole. But don't you dare come. This one is for me." I shove her back down but don't loosen my grip on her hair. She uses the banister as leverage to piston back and forth on my girth, tightening her Kegels with every backward thrust, eliciting a curse from my lips. "That's right, baby. Fuck, you should see how your tight cunt swallows my cock." She whimpers at my dirty words, and her movements stutter as she works to bring her orgasm forward. I chastise her with another slap to her ass. "Don't you fucking dare, Camil Greco." She impales herself on my cock with a maddening pace, and though I'm sore as hell, I wouldn't stop this for the world because my girl needs this, and fuck if I don't need it too.

Too soon, my balls draw up, and my tailbone tingles with my impending release. Taking over, I grip her hips with a bruising hold and shove myself so deep I know it has to hurt, but Camil just moans and tightens around me because she knows what that does to me. I howl her name as I fill her with my seed and swear to Christ, my eyes cloud with tears. So damn good.

I slowly withdraw from her warmth and then put myself back together before cleaning her up and helping her to dress. In typical Texas style, the weather went from a balmy seventy-five degrees Fahrenheit to forty, then to below-freezing and snowing, and has been for the last three days. It reminds me of what one of the guys in my unit who was born and raised here said, *Texas always has one last cold snap in late February or early March.*

Camil pouted the entire day when the weather turned, and the first flutter of snowflakes covered the grass. She wanted the heat she had heard about, but then the little girl inside her remembered the times she used her big gray eyes to manipulate Emil and me into snowball fights with her; of course, she always reigned victorious. Then we would go inside, where Emil's mother would make us hot cocoa and tell us stories of snow princesses and white knights––until Idris would come in and tell her to stop filling our minds with ridiculous fairy tales.

"I really can't go out to the mailbox? That seems a bit extreme, Bo," Camil complains.

I help her pull on her cardigan, then pull her into my arms. "As long as there's still a threat out there, I need you to stay out of sight. It's bad enough that the guys and I have to leave you to go fix the breach on the south side of our land."

She bites her bottom lip and smiles. "Our land?"

I squeeze her tighter to me. "Yes, *our* land. You're my wife now. But even if you weren't, everything I have is yours, Camil." Her brow puckers in confusion, so I explain. "The day I enlisted, I had our lawyers write up my will and had everything go to you if I didn't make it out alive." She winces at the latter, but I press forward. "I wanted you to have a way out of this life if that's what you wanted, and that hasn't changed. You will have my money, my properties, even my men."

She brushes a lock of hair from my forehead and looks at me with so much love that my knees nearly buckle under its weight. "So even in death, you will protect me."

"*Sempre* (always)," I promise. But that's the thing about promises. They can be broken... even if we don't mean to break them.

29

Camil

"I can't believe it's finally here," Greta frets from the other side of the seventy-inch T.V. screen Boian set up to broadcast Emil and Greta's wedding. It's not ideal, but it will have to do.

"You act like you've been waiting six months rather than one." I giggle and laugh harder when she brings her face so close to the camera I can see up her nose.

"Don't you dare take this freak out from me, Camil Greco. Everything happened so fast that I didn't get to be a true bridezilla, so give me this."

"Come on, Greta. There is no way you would be a bridezilla. You didn't give a damn about one thing that had to do with the wedding. You might as well have been the man."

She leans away from the camera and puckers her lips in contemplation. "True. Okay, maybe I wouldn't have been horrible, but I am actually nervous. I just..." She chokes up, and I wait for her to compose herself. "I love him so much, and I know he's a wicked man."

She smiles, and I return it with my own, letting her know I understand. "But he's *my* wicked man, and I can't help but love him."

"Greta, you don't have to explain or justify yourself to anyone. Our men aren't saints, but they're not heartless either. Though they would argue otherwise, they have some of the biggest hearts I've ever seen. Just *keep* loving him."

She sighs dreamily. "I don't think I have any other choice, and this is the one time I'm okay with that fact."

Her phone chimes with a reminder, and she jumps up, nearly knocking over the camera. "Okay, girl, it's your time to shine. Boian and I will be right there with you."

"Okay, okay. Okay." She's completely frazzled, and I can't help but laugh as I click over to the ceremony feed where Emil stands at the altar in a dark suit, sans tie, his hands clasped in front of him, and it pains me to see him with no one by his side.

Boian and I should be there, but I ruined it.

Mentally shaking myself, I shut down those negative thoughts and smile at the man I consider a brother. He glances at the screen and lifts a pinky in acknowledgment, and that one little gesture sends warmth through my chest and thankful tears to my eyes.

As the wedding procession begins, Boian comes charging through the front door and, without so much as a hello, plops next to me and pulls me into his arms, where I blubber the entire time our friends promise themselves to one another.

When Emil and Greta turn to face the small gathering of people, they look into the camera with broad smiles, and Boian snaps a shot of them. Greta blows me a kiss before they both disappear behind the camera and against my best efforts, my mood sours.

Ever observant, Boian catches the shift in mood and tips my chin up until our eyes meet. My gray and self-loathing to his violet and stern. "Stop it," he scolds. "What's done is done. Besides, those two wouldn't even notice if the sky was raining down balls of fire right now, they're so happy."

He doesn't try to patronize me by saying it's not my fault, and though it stings, I adore him for it. He promised he wouldn't lie to me, and so far, he's holding true to that promise.

"I know, but that's now two weddings I didn't get to be a part of," I mumble with a bite of resentment. So, maybe I'm still a little miffed at him for forging my name and making me his wife without a chance to say the treasured "I do's."

He pulls me onto his lap, and I smother my face into his neck to get a hit of his leather and sandalwood scent. *"Perdonami, mio fiore."* Forgive me, my flower. "I shouldn't have gone about it as I did, and I won't insult your intelligence by trying to justify it."

I inhale his familiar scent, and the resentment melts away like ice cream on a summer day in Texas. "We both messed up––did stupid stuff. I just want to move on," I say and find myself meaning it. I want to be done with all the regrets and resentment. It's all a waste of our precious time on this earth.

Boian strokes my hair and kisses my head. "You will have the wedding you've always wanted, *fiore*. Let's focus on neutralizing this threat, and then I will give you the world."

I snuggle closer and kiss his Adam's apple. "I don't need the world, Bo. Just you."

"Done," he answers and snuggles me closer. Too soon, our little bubble of peace is broken when Dom walks in, and Boian has to leave to fix the fence breach. Apparently, a coyote got caught in the snowstorm and came onto our land to find shelter in the ramshackle shed Boian planned to convert into a "she shed" for me. Unfortunately, the poor thing got caught in the wire, triggering the silent alarm. Boian was able to free the poor animal, but the line had been compromised and couldn't be repaired until the snow had melted enough. But the fact that it requires all three of them to repair put the guys on edge.

A point Boian reminds me of when he leans into me to place a kiss on my forehead. "Stay inside," he warns, and I grin at him mischievously.

"No promises," I return and get a beastly growl from him that has my core tingling and my nipples tightening.

While the men do their thing, I slob out on the couch and start my Monster: The Jeffrey Dahmer story marathon everyone is raving about. I'm at the episode where Dahmer is sent to the army when a shadow passes across the beam of sunshine coming through the window. Instantly my survival instincts are on alert, and I slowly slide from the couch to lie belly down on the floor. I army crawl to the window and peek out to see a tall Hispanic man standing at the door. His jaw is covered in a dark, neatly trimmed beard, his skin tan, his eyes the color of summer grass, and tattoos that peek out from beneath the collar of his heavy jacket. My gut screams that the man is not one of Boian's or an unexpected guard sent by Emil.

This is not good.

I jump when a heavy knock sounds against the steel door. I have a possible enemy at my door—an enemy that knocks oddly enough. Okay, that doesn't make sense, but I'll be damned if I'm going to open the door.

My instincts are proven correct when the man calls out in a lightly accented voice, "Caaamil," the man taunts. "Come out, come out wherever you are. Or don't. I love a good hunt, *pequeño.*"

A scraping sound comes from the small window by the door, then the familiar beep indicating that the person has gained entry.

"Shit," I whisper and leap to my feet to follow the escape protocol the guys put in place. Oddly enough, it's not much different from the one I executed in Romania to escape Boian—let's just hope I have better luck this time.

I quietly but quickly race to the seamless attic door, pull down the ladder, and climb up as swiftly but silently as possible. The door is well-oiled and shuts without a single creak. I bear-crawl to the hidden access door on the side of the house where the two levels connect, climb down the roof, then jump down into the soft powder of snow below.

"Don't move, little one," the man says directly behind me.

How the hell did he find me? Who cares, Camil? Run!

The crunch of the man's boot sinking into the snow puts my legs in motion. I sprint down the path we shoveled for this exact situation. Unfortunately, it aids my pursuer as well as I hear him take chase, and one thing becomes clear. He hasn't shot me—which means he needs me alive. With that in mind, I smile and push my legs to their limit. I may be small, but I'm quick, and soon I feel the distance grow between my would-be captor and me.

I hit the unkempt part of the tree line where the utility cart waits hidden in the foliage just a few yards away. The man's thundering footfalls tell me he's getting closer, but I don't stop until I come to the decaying trunk of a fallen tree. The limbs are void of leaves, but the massive tree camouflages the small cavern behind it. With one last look behind me, I confirm that the man is no longer in sight, so I grab a thick broken limb and toss it and craggy pieces of stems and leaves over my footpath before scrambling over the trunk and entering the cave's small opening.

My breaths become heavy but steady as I sit curled against the freezing cave wall, listening as leaves crunch and sticks crack under the man's heavy steps. "You're only delaying the inevitable, *pequeño*. It took me a long time to find his weakness."

Who is talking about?

Even as I ask myself the question, I know the answer before the man speaks again. "Greco will pay for what he did. My brother was weak and a sick *cabrón,* but his wife and children did not deserve to die." I clamp a hand over my mouth to keep a gasp from slipping from my lips. This is about the mission in Mexico.

"My niece and nephew were innocent, and their deaths must be avenged little one." He speaks as though he's having a casual conversation with a friend and not coming to kidnap a woman as revenge.

Boian's words come back to me at that moment. The man they were after sold women and children into slavery. Dear God, is that what this man plans to do––sell me as revenge?

I don't get to ponder that horrifying thought for long when my arm is grabbed and I'm dragged from my hiding spot. The man brings me face to face with him, and my eyes go immediately to the long, jagged scar running horizontally across his forehead.

"Hello, Camil Radu." He smiles. "My apologies. It's Camil Greco now, isn't it?" I gasp, and my eyes widen in horror. "That's right, little one. I know all about you."

30

Boian

Repairing the breach is taking too long, and each second we spend out here instead of at the house watching over Camil is a second too long.

We've just finished uploading the code for the new sensor when another alarm sounds through our phones. "Fuck!" I growl and take off like an Olympic sprinter toward the house, fear I've never felt before racing like acid through my veins. "Dom, go around the back. Lorenzo, watch the perimeter. I'm going through the front," I tell the men through the comms Lorenzo insisted we wear in case of such an instance.

"*Sí*, Boss," they answer in unison.

I approach the house but stop in my tracks when I see the front door wide open. "Fuck," I curse and pull my gun from my waistband. "The front door's been hacked," I update the guys. "Camil!" I shout into the house and feel my stomach revolt when I'm met with silence.

"I don't think she's home, Boss. The attic trap door is open, and footprints on the roof and below lead to the forest. Looks like she followed the protocol."

Good girl.

"Lorenzo, Dom, head into the forest. I'm right behind you," I command, and like a well-oiled machine, we move as one and split off. I head for the thickest part of the forest where Camil was instructed to go. At the same time, Lorenzo and Dom follow the fence line.

My boot breaches the tree line right as Camil's shouted cursing comes from deep within the forest. Without hesitation, I sprint forward, gun at the ready, as Camil's screams become muffled. At the same time, a string of Spanish, growled in a deep masculine voice, competes with her bellows.

"You are not getting away, little one," the man says, and I stop to scan the surrounding area but don't see any movement. The voices are bouncing off the trees, throwing off their location.

BANG.

A shot goes off, and suddenly Camil's shouts go silent, and with it, my heart. My knees buckle, and I have to use the tree beside me to keep me upright.

"Boian!" Dom's voice calls through the comms, along with the distant sound of an engine revving, but it all fades to static in my ears as I die where I stand.

"Boian, he's getting away, and he has Camil!" Lorenzo's words finally penetrate the fog of despair, and my head whips up and swings on a swivel, looking for any sign of the man that has my wife.

"Where the fuck are you?" I grit through the comms.

"Northeast end of the forest. Look for the rocks," Lorenzo instructs before more shots go off. I swing my head toward the sound of gunfire and barely see the tip of a large rock formation. I take flight, pushing my legs to the edge of exhaustion. But when I come up on the cliff, Dom and Lorenzo are racing back in my direction, guns at their sides and murderous looks on their faces.

"What the fuck happened?" I grumble through a tight throat and a now rapid heartbeat.

"Camil and some fucker were struggling, but I was too far away and couldn't risk hitting Camil, so I fired a warning shot, and the guy..." Lorenzo trails off.

"The guy what? Spit it out!"

"He hit Camil and knocked her out, then took off. We were closing in on him when a four-wheeler came racing out of nowhere. He jumped on with her and then sped off." Lorenzo's hand flexes around his gun while Dom stands staring into the distance, tapping his weapon against his thigh.

I turn in circles and run a shaky hand through my hair. Desperation, fear, and rage claw at my chest because, for the first time in my life, I don't know what my next move is, and it's fucking eating me alive. Steadying myself, I release an icy breath before turning and racing to the SUV waiting outside the house.

"The man spoke Spanish. Look into any beefs with the cartels."

"The *famiglia* doesn't work with the cartels, Boss."

"I'm aware of that. Do it anyway. Get with gaming and wildlife officers too. See if they have any information on the four-wheeler. I doubt they brought it with them."

"We're on it. Who's calling Emil?" Lorenzo asks when we reach the SUV.

I swing the door open and settle into the front passenger seat, Lorenzo at the wheel and Dom in the back, still silent and contemplative. "I'll call the don. This fucker just declared war on the *famiglia*. I hope you two are ready for this?" I swing my eyes to Dom in the back seat.

"I'm always ready to gut a motherfucker for messing with our family," he answers without looking at me. I nod, then look back at Lorenzo.

"You know I'm always up for a good slice and dice, Boss." He gives me a wicked smirk, and with a stomp of his foot on the accelerator, we take chase.

I'm about to dial Emil when my cell phone lights up with Alexander's, my man on the street's, name. I connect the call. "Now is not the time, Alex. We have––"

"Does Sinaloa, Mexico ring a bell?" My breath sticks in my lungs, and my heart misses a beat at the name of that Godforsaken city.

My vision clouds with the scene of that doomed day in Mexico. The bloody and battered women and children could barely stand to walk from the building. I can still feel the heat of the explosion on my face and the feeling of guilt, remorse, and self-disgust when I found out I killed that woman and her kids.

"Boss?" Alexander's deep grumble sounds through the Bluetooth.

"You all right, Boss?" This time it's Dom that asks, and I have to pull myself from the living nightmare playing out in my head and level out my breathing before I answer.

"I was on assignment there for a while back in my military days. Why?" I ask, but he doesn't need to answer for me to know what he's going to say.

"Word on the street is that the brother of the man you killed during that assignment is out for blood. Something about a woman and her kids caught in the crossfire."

"It wasn't crossfire. It was a fucking explosion." I run a trembling hand through my hair and decide to come clean. "An explosion I pressed the detonator on." I'm met with silence at my confession. "Now we know the who and why," I continue. "We need the where because the fucker just took Camil."

"Fuck," Alexander mumbles to himself.

"Fuck is right. As in, they're fucking with the wrong *famiglia*."

"A war with the cartel? This is going to get bloody."

"Yes, it is," I agree. "Let the battle commence."

To be Continued

Turn the page to get a sneak peek at the fourth and final book in the Roma series,

The Roma's Vow

Sneak Peek: The Roma's Vow

Camil

"E*sta no es una guerra que podamos ganar."*
This is not a war we can win.

"Cállate!" Shut up!

The men bicker back and forth, and it's starting to grate on my already thread-thin nerves. We've been driving for thirty minutes, and my head hasn't stopped thumping from the hit to my temple. Add these two *bastardo's* back-and-forth bitching, and you have a woman one gun short of killing someone.

The men's voices rise, and the thread snaps. *"Ambos se callan!"* I groan in Spanish, and both men's heads swing my way, their eyes wide in surprise before the driver turns back to the road ahead.

"You're full of surprises, *pequeño*," the passenger says as he smiles back at me with mossy green eyes, shaggy black hair, and a trimmed beard to match. The only thing flawing his handsome face is the long, jagged scar running horizontally along his forehead to stop at the tip of his right eyebrow. The man notices me staring at the blemished skin and runs a long finger across it. "You should see the other guy," he quips and turns back to face the front.

"Who are you?" I catch the driver's eyes in the review mirror, but it's his friend in the passenger seat who speaks up. "My apologies, Mrs. Greco," he answers before he turns back to me and places a hand on his chest, and I have to school my features at the reminder that he knows Boian and I are married. "I am Hector Ramos, and this *cabrón* is my cousin Jose."

"And why exactly am I in this disgusting van heading to who knows where, Hector?"

"I'm sorry it's not a stretch limousine, *Camil,* but we have to stay under the radar. You understand, don't you? And as for where we are going? That's on a need-to-know basis." He gives me a toothy grin.

"And the other part?" He tilts his head in question. "Why?" I clarify.

Hector chuckles and looks at me like I'm an idiot. "Come now, Camil. You are friends with the most powerful man in Europe. Surely this isn't the first time you've been kidnapped," he deadpans, but I find nothing funny about the situation.

"It is, actually. And you're full of shit, Ramos."

"Meaning?" he asks with a quirk of a dark brow.

"Meaning Emil doesn't involve himself with the cartel. He's always been respectful of their claim in the States. So, your beef isn't with him."

The mocking smirk turns to one of surprise and ... respect? "You're a very smart woman, Mrs. Greco. You're right. I have no problem with Emiliano Calvano. It's your husband I'm after."

My stomach drops, but I refuse to show emotion. "Boian is not my husband. He's my ... nothing," I lie to see how much the man knows.

Again, Hector chuckles. "Even if that were true—— which it is not——the man cares for you as someone would for a person he's grown up protecting. That alone is enough."

My heart dances a chaotic rhythm in my chest, and I have to swallow the fear clogging my throat. "How do you know so much about my family, and why are you going after Boian?" I already know his reason for taking me, but I need to try and get as much information as possible from him. I'm unsure how long I was knocked out, and I don't know where we are.

"I suppose it won't hurt to tell you. Your lov... husband killed my brother, his wife, and two kids. My niece and nephew." His green eyes turn nearly pitch black, and I remember his words as I hid in the shallow cavern.

Greco will pay for what he did. My brother was weak and a sick cabrón, but his wife and children did not deserve to die.

Bile creeps up my throat, and I wince at the acidic sting. "Boian killed your brother because your brother deserved it."

"And his wife and children?" Hector snarls.

"Boian didn't intentionally kill them," I argue vehemently.

"Are you sure? Do you know the things he was paid to do?"

"Paid?" I ask before I can stop myself.

"Ah, now I see. You didn't know your husband was a paid mercenary for the American government." He chuckles triumphantly, and I have to blink away the stinging tears of disappointment.

When Boian and Emil went into the Italian forces, I was angry that they were leaving me, but proud of them once I got over the initial hurt. They were fighting to keep our country safe. So, how did Boian get involved with the American government as a paid killer?

I know it's hypocritical of me because, as a member of the *famiglia*, Boian has killed before, but with one glaring difference––Boian doesn't hurt women and children. At least not intentionally.

"Maybe so. But what happened with your brother's family was an accident. And yes, I am sure of that."

Hector nods and turns back to the front. "You may be right, little one. Regardless, he's the one that pushed the button that leveled my brother's compound and my niece and nephew with it." My stomach knots, and tears clog my throat at the thought of those terrified children clinging to their mother. I can only pray it happened so quickly that there was no pain.

Jesus, I live in a fucked-up world.

We pull into an airplane hangar with rows of private jets, and my heart pinches when I don't see the Calvano crest on any of them.

The van door creaks open. "Let's go." Hector waves me from the van. I step onto the tarmac covered in powdery snow and smile.

"They're not going to let us fly out of here. There has to be at least a foot of snow on the runway."

Hector smiles condescendingly and taps the tip of my nose. "You'd be surprised what money can buy you." Of course, he bought his getaway.

I sigh. "Not really," I throw back.

"The runway we'll be using has been cleared, and the plane is ready. So, little one, it's time to go. Are you going to go peacefully, or do we need to sedate you like a yippy little Pomeranian?" He grins, and my fist flies before I can talk any sense into myself.

My knuckles connect with Hector's chiseled jaw, sending a painful bolt of electricity through my hand and up my arm, but I refuse to wince or shake out my hand. Not that I get a chance because Hector's hand is in my hair, fisting the roots to the point of pain before my next inhale. His eyes turn maniacal, and he bares his teeth like a rabid animal. "You will *never* hit me again," he growls in my face.

"Wanna bet?" I return with my own growl, then grunt when he spins me with my hair still in his grasp and shoves me against the side of the van. My cheek instantly chills from the cold steel pressed against it.

"Don't test me, little one. You have no idea how far my reach goes. I have spent years watching you, your precious Boian, and everyone close to you. That includes his boss ... and his precious *perla*." My eyes widen, and fear digs its claws into flesh and bone.

"Fine! I'll go. I won't touch you again," I grit through tears of rage and terror.

He runs the tip of his nose against my temple and smiles wickedly. "I didn't say I don't want you to touch me," he purrs on a grind of his erection into my lower back. I gasp at the feel of him and mentally curse myself when he chuckles lowly in my ear. "Now apologize," he orders, then tugs sharply on my hair when I don't respond.

"Ugh, I'm sorry!"

He releases my hair and then brings his lips to the side of my cheek. "Good girl," he whispers against my skin, and I shiver at those words because only one other man has called me a good girl, and I'm terrified I will never hear my violet-eyed beast whisper those words to me again.

Book Club Questions

1. What was your favorite part of the book?

2. What was your least favorite?

3. Did you race to the end, or was it more of a slow burn?

4. Which scene has stuck with you the most?

5. What did you think of the writing? Are there any standout sentences?

6. Did you reread any passages? If so, which ones?

7. Would you want to read another book by this author?

8. Did reading the book impact your mood? If yes, how so?

9. What surprised you most about the book?

10. How did your opinion of the book change as you read it?

SHAE COON

Award-winning author Shae Coon writes dark romance that tantalizes while leaving you guessing what comes next. Her inspiration came from author Penelope Sky after reading her Buttons and Lace series and fell in love with the angsty alpha males and twisted plot lines. Shae has eight published titles, including the Marron House Romance Series and the Dark Roma Mafia Romance Series.

Before she started writing romance, Shae received her veterinary assistant certification and worked in a low-cost vet clinic before switching gears to become the top-performing project coordinator for a local construction company and ultimately leaving to pursue her dream of becoming a full-time writer.

Shae is a die-hard Dallas Stars hockey fan who enjoys iced coffee, books, and spending time with her crazy, outspoken, say-it-as-it-is family. Shae also volunteers her time to other authors, whether helping them with imposter syndrome, creating a beautiful book cover for an up-and-coming author, or interviewing them to help get the word out.

When Shae is not writing, you will find her coaching her daughter's basketball team, volunteering with an anti-human trafficking organization, or relaxing with her husband and two children.

Now, go be naughty.

More books from
4 Horsemen Publications

Erotica

Ali Whippe
Office Hours
Tutoring Center
Athletics
Extra Credit
Financial Aid
Bound for Release
Fetish Circuit
Now You See Me
Sexual Playground
Swingers
Discovered
XTC College Series Collection

Aria Skylar
Twisted Eros
Seducing Dionysus

Chastity Veldt
Molly in Milwaukee
Irene in Indianapolis
Lydia in Louisville
Natasha in Nashville
Alyssa in Atlanta
Betty in Birmingham
Carrie on Campus

Jackie in Jacksonville
A Humorous Erotica Collection

Dalia Lance
My Home on Whore Island
Slumming It on Slut Street
Training of the Tramp
The Imperfect Perfection
Spring Break
72% Match
It Was Meant To Be...
Or Whatever

Honey Cummings
Sleeping with Sasquatch
Cuddling with Chupacabra
Naked with New Jersey Devil
Laying with the Lady in Blue
Wanton Woman in White
Beating it with Bloody Mary
The Erotic Cryptid Collection
Beau and Professor Bestialora
The Goat's Gruff
Goldie and Her Three Beards
Pied Piper's Pipe
Princess Pea's Bed
Pinocchio and the Blow Up Doll

Jack's Beanstalk

Pulling Rapunzel's Hair

The Urban Erotica Fairy Tale
Collection

Curses & Crushes

Queen's Incubus

Nick Savage

The Fairlane Incidents

The Fortunate Finn Fairlane

The Fragile Finn Fairlane

The Complete Package

Nova Embers

A Game of Sales

How Marketing Beats Dick

Certified Public Alpha (CPA)

On the Job Experience

My GIF is Bigger than Your GIF

Power Play

Plugging in My USB

Hunting the White Elephant

Caution: Slippery When Wet

ROMANCE

Ann Shepphird

The War Council

Emily Bunney

All or Nothing

All the Way

All Night Long: Novella

All She Needs

Having it All

All at Once

All Together

All for Her

KT Bond

Back to Life

Back to Love

Back at Last

Lynn Chantale

The Baker's Touch

Blind Secrets

Broken Lens

Blind Fury

Time Bomb

VIP's Revenge

Chef's Taste

The Gold Standard

DISCOVER MORE AT
4HORSEMENPUBLICATIONS.COM

Printed in the USA
CPSIA information can be obtained
at www.ICGtesting.com
LVHW041757280923
759519LV00005B/80